"You must be Santiago Jones."

"That's me," Jones said. "I've got an idea, Adams."

"What's that?"

"Why don't we step down from our horses and settle this between us?"

"That sounds good to me."

"Your man will stay out of it?"

"He will. And yours?"

"They will, too."

"Okay, then," Clint said. "Step down."

"Is he serious?" Coleman asked.

"No," Clint said. "Watch the others. They'll draw, for sure."

"I don't know . . ."

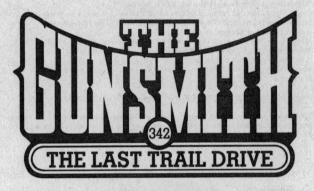

# THE GUNSMITH

## 342

## THE LAST TRAIL DRIVE

## J. R. ROBERTS

JOVE BOOKS, NEW YORK

**THE BERKLEY PUBLISHING GROUP**
**Published by the Penguin Group**
**Penguin Group (USA) Inc.**
**375 Hudson Street, New York, New York 10014, USA**
Penguin Group (Canada), 90 Eglinton Avenue East, Suite 700, Toronto, Ontario M4P 2Y3, Canada
(a division of Pearson Penguin Canada Inc.)
Penguin Books Ltd., 80 Strand, London WC2R 0RL, England
Penguin Group Ireland, 25 St. Stephen's Green, Dublin 2, Ireland (a division of Penguin Books Ltd.)
Penguin Group (Australia), 250 Camberwell Road, Camberwell, Victoria 3124, Australia
(a division of Pearson Australia Group Pty. Ltd.)
Penguin Books India Pvt. Ltd., 11 Community Centre, Panchsheel Park, New Delhi—110 017, India
Penguin Group (NZ), 67 Apollo Drive, Rosedale, North Shore 0632, New Zealand
(a division of Pearson New Zealand Ltd.)
Penguin Books (South Africa) (Pty.) Ltd., 24 Sturdee Avenue, Rosebank, Johannesburg 2196,
South Africa

Penguin Books Ltd., Registered Offices: 80 Strand, London WC2R 0RL, England

This is a work of fiction. Names, characters, places, and incidents either are the product of the author's imagination or are used fictitiously, and any resemblance to actual persons, living or dead, business establishments, events, or locales is entirely coincidental.

THE LAST TRAIL DRIVE

A Jove Book / published by arrangement with the author

PRINTING HISTORY
Jove edition / June 2010

ISBN: 978-0-515-14809-1

JOVE®
Jove Books are published by The Berkley Publishing Group,
a division of Penguin Group (USA) Inc.,
375 Hudson Street, New York, New York 10014.
JOVE® is a registered trademark of Penguin Group (USA) Inc.
The "J" design is a trademark of Penguin Group (USA) Inc.

PRINTED IN THE UNITED STATES OF AMERICA

10  9  8  7  6  5  4  3  2  1

# ONE

Doan's Crossing, in the Texas Panhandle, was once the jumping-off place for trail drives heading north to Colorado and Montana. As Clint Adams rode into town he could see it had fallen on hard times. Trail drives were not a commonplace occurrence anymore. Towns that once depended on them for their livelihoods—Dodge City, Ellsworth, Doan's Crossing—were dying.

Clint was not in Doan's Crossing for old times' sake, though. He was there to meet a friend of his, an old-time trail boss named Flood. He didn't know why Flood wanted to meet him, or why he wanted to meet in this town, but they were good enough friends that he came anyway.

He had ridden to the Panhandle directly from Labyrinth, Texas, arriving exactly on the day he and Flood were to meet. He hadn't seen Henry Flood in five years. Flood was fifty then, and was lamenting the oncoming end of the great trail drives. Flood was smart enough to see how the railroad was spreading, and soon drives would not be necessary to move cattle. Also, the advent of barbed wire, and the invention of Gustavus Swift's refrigerated car, were pretty much sealing the deal.

The reason Flood wanted Clint to meet him here, where

many of the man's cattle drive's had pushed off, had to have something to do with cattle, but what? Clint had ridden in from the south and had seen neither hide nor hail of a steer. He was just going to have to wait for Flood to arrive to find out.

Clint saw to it that Eclipse was well cared for at a livery stable, and then got himself a room at the Central Hotel. He checked with the clerk, but no one named Flood had checked in yet.

He stowed his things in his room, and then went to the Crystal Palace Saloon. Once a thriving saloon and gaming establishment, it had obviously fallen on hard times. It was early, but that was not the reason there was no gambling going on. As he entered he saw that all the gaming tables that had once filled the place were gone. In their place were empty tables and chairs.

Clint went to the bar, where a barman was fighting boredom by wiping the bar down with a dirty rag. When he saw Clint, he slung the rag over his shoulder.

"Help ya?"

"Beer."

"Right."

The man brought Clint a beer that was warm and had too much head.

"That the best you can do?" Clint asked.

"Best I can do," the barman said, "and best you're gonna get in town."

"Glad I'm just passing through then," Clint said.

"Least it's wet."

Clint took a sip, and decided that was all that could be said for the beer—it was wet.

"Days of cold beer are gone, I'm afraid," the barman said. "Left with the cattle drives, I guess."

"How long you been a barman?" Clint asked.

The man grinned.

"Since the cattle drives left," he said.

"Drover?"

"Cook, if you can believe it," the man said. "I know, I look more like a waddie."

Clint studied the man. He was tall, about six three, looked fit, except for a slight potbelly. Had the look of a waddie more than a cook. In his forties, he was still capable of participating in a cattle drive . . . if he could find one. A *waddie* used to be called a rustler, but as the years went on became known as a cowboy who moved from outfit to outfit, working cattle drives.

"Came here a few years ago looking to hook up with some outfit," he said. "Never did. Took this job as a temporary thing." He laughed. "Temporary."

"When was the last drive that came through here?" Clint asked.

"'Bout one or two each year the last few years, but they wasn't hirin'," the barman said.

"You know a man named Henry Flood? Hank—Hank Flood?" Clint asked.

"Flood? Don't know 'im, but heard of 'im."

"Heard of him lately? Here in town?"

"No, not lately," the barman said. "Why? You lookin' for him?"

"He's looking for me," Clint said.

The man stuck out a large hand.

"Name's Spud," he said. "Spud Johnson."

"Spud?"

The man grinned.

"I can do wonders with a potato."

Clint shook his hand and said, "Clint Adams."

"Clint . . . Adams?" Spud asked.

"That's right."

"You friends with Flood, Mr. Adams?" Spud asked.

"I am," Clint said. "Long time."

"So you're not here for . . . I mean, to cause . . . um, I mean, to kill—"

"Don't believe everything you read or hear, Spud," Clint said. "I don't go anywhere to kill anyone. Understand?"

"Oh, yessir," Spud said. "I understand good."

"Calm down," Clint said, as the man grew tense. "There's nothing to be nervous about. The only thing I'm here to kill is some time over a warm beer."

"Yessir."

"I'm going to take a turn around town," Clint said. "If Hank Flood does come in looking for me tell him to stay put. I'll find him."

"I'll do it, Mr. Adams."

"It's Clint, Spud," Clint said. "It's just Clint. Okay?"

"Yessir," the barman said. "That's okay with me."

# TWO

There was one other saloon in operation in Doan's Crossing. There used to be more, but one by one they had gone out of business. There also used to be a number of whorehouses, but now there was just one.

Debra Moore remembered when the trail drives used to come to town—or, more to the point, the drovers. They used to come to the whorehouses by the dozens, trying to get their ashes hauled one last time before they hit the trail for three months. Some men found it nearly impossible to go that long without a woman.

She thought three months without hearing another woman's voice, or seeing another woman, would have been paradise. Debra was popular with men, but other women hated her, and it was mutual.

When she was younger they used to hate her because she was so pretty. Now that she was in her thirties, they hated her because she so obviously had distain for all of them.

In other words, she had an attitude.

She stood on the balcony smoking a cigarette, the wrap she was wearing barely hiding her opulent curves. Men rode by and stared up at her. Women glared.

The door behind her opened, and someone came out.

"Got a fella for you." It was Glenda, the madam, an old whore who had stayed around long enough to be put in charge. She was fat and fifty, and hated not only Debra but all the other whores who were younger than she was.

"Give him to one of the other girls," she said. "I'm on a break. And my pussy's sore."

"Yeah, all the girls got sore pussies," Glenda said. "Mine's still sore from thirty years on my back."

Debra grinned at Glenda and said, "I'm surprised you still have a pussy."

"Smart mouth," Glenda said. "How about you get inside and put your smart mouth to work?"

"I told you, give him to one of the other girls."

"He don't want one of the other girls, he wants you," Glenda said.

"He asked for me?"

"Yeah."

"Who is it?"

"How do I know?" Glenda said. "Just some cowboy."

Debra drew on her cigarette, then flicked it out into the street down below.

"If you don't want to work, Debra, why don't you pack up and leave town?"

"Don't worry, Glenda," Debra said, "I will, and soon. This town's about a week from dead."

"Get inside before your cowboy walks out the door with his money."

"And goes where?" Debra asked. "Where else is he gonna go and get a poke in this town?"

"Maybe a friendly saloon girl."

"The saloon girls in this town are hags."

"That may be, but they got wet slits between their legs, just like we got—well, maybe not you anymore. You dried up a long time ago, didn't you, Glen?"

"Bitch!" Glenda said, and left Debra standing there.

* * *

Before Debra went inside she lit another cigarette and smoked it slowly. As she did she saw a man in the street stop and look up at her. Even at a distance she could tell this was not a man like other men. It was in his stature. This was not a man she was ever likely to meet while plying her trade. This man didn't need to pay for a woman. Women were drawn to him.

But not this woman, she thought, shaking her head and flicking another cigarette into the street.

This woman had work to do.

Glenda found the cowboy waiting in the hall.

"She'll be down soon, cowboy," she said.

"Thank you, Ma'am."

"You sure you don't wanna try one of the other, younger girls?"

"No, thank you, Ma'am," the man said, fingering his hat in his hands, "I'll just wait for Debra."

Glenda shook her head and said. "Suit yerself."

Debra went back inside, walked downstairs, and found the cowboy waiting for her in the front hall.

"Hello, Deb," he said.

She stared at him and said, "Sonofabitch."

He grinned at her.

"Good," he said. "You still remember me. Now how 'bout we go upstairs?"

"Fuck you, Roy," she said.

"That's kinda what I had in mind."

# THREE

Henry Flood rode into town with his segundo, Jack Trevor. Just outside of town to the east was a herd of a thousand Texas beeves. His hands were busy branding them, getting them ready for the drive North.

"Just like old times, huh, Hank?" Trevor said.

"Not quite, Jack," Flood said. "This town looks all but dead."

"Yeah," Trevor said, "I remember how it used to be. But still . . . it's Doan's Crossing, huh? Let's get a drink."

"Okay, we'll get a drink, but then we got to find us a cook, and we got to find us a Gunsmith."

"Hank," Trevor asked, "what do we need with the Gunsmith?"

"The man's a legend, Jack."

"Yeah, maybe, but he ain't a drover."

"He don't have to be," Flood said. "He's my friend. And this just might be the last trail drive. We need to have a legend along with us."

"But Hank . . . you're a legend."

"I ain't a legend, Jack," Flood said. "I'm a tired-out old trail boss."

Flood was probably sixty, but it was hard to tell. His face

was lined, but that could have been from the sand and sun, not from age. He spent most of his life on the trail, at the mercy of the elements.

Jack Trevor had been riding with Flood for the past twenty years. He joined him as a very young man, learned his trade, and was now a top number two man—the best of the foreman—and maybe the last.

"You're the best trail boss there ever was, Boss," Trevor said.

"So then, I must know what I'm doin', right?" Flood asked.

"Yeah, right."

Flood reined in his horse in front of the Crystal Saloon.

"Let's get that drink, and then we can start lookin'. I wanna get that herd started tomorrow."

They dismounted.

"You think we're gonna find us a cook in one day?" Trevor asked.

"We're either gonna find one," Flood said, "or I'm gonna do the cookin' myself."

Clint had been in the saddle for days, so a walk around town was good for stretching his legs. It was also sad, because a lot of storefronts were closed and boarded up. The once thriving Doan's Crossing had fallen on the same hard times as many other towns along the old Chisum and Goodnight-Loving Trails.

He passed one building that was not boarded up. Up on a second-floor balcony a woman was standing, slowly smoking a cigarette. She was wearing just enough clothing to cover her body, but he could tell from where he was that she was generously built.

He knew she was watching him. She stood confidently, and if he was in the habit of frequenting cathouses he would have gone right in and asked for her. But he didn't pay for women, so that wasn't going to happen.

She flicked her cigarette into the street. It arced, leaving a trail of sparks behind it, and then landed in the street. By the time he looked up again, she was gone from the balcony.

# FOUR

Flood and Jack Trevor each had two beers, despite the fact they weren't cold. The saloon was empty, another indication of how Doan's Crossing had fallen on hard times.

"This place used to be alive all the time," Jack Trevor remembered. "Now it just seems dead."

"I know how it feels," Flood said.

"What does that mean?"

Flood shrugged.

"Just that I know what it means to feel dead inside," Flood said.

"What are you talkin' about, Boss?"

Flood leaned both elbows on the top of the bar.

"I'm tired, Jack," Flood said. "Tired and just about done."

"But we got a drive, Boss," Trevor said. "That'll make ya feel alive again."

"It probably will, but it'll end, too," Flood said. "This could be my last trail drive, Jack. It might also be the last trail drive ever."

"Well, that may be okay for you," Trevor said, "but what about me and the other boys?"

"You're all young enough to do somethin' else with your

lives, Jack," Flood said. "Hell, you boys are gonna be alive to see a new century."

"It ain't that far off, Boss," Trevor said. "You'll be around, too."

"Christ," Trevor said, "I'll be near seventy. Don't know that I ever wanna get that old. I'd rather just die on the trail."

Trevor straightened up and stood square to his boss, facing him.

"Is that was this is about, Boss?" he demanded. "You lookin' ta die on this drive?"

Flood looked at the younger man and said, "Hell no, Jack! What the hell are you talkin' about, boy?"

"You're the one talkin' about how you're gonna die," Trevor shot back.

"Yeah, but not for a while," Flood said. "I still got some life left in me, boy. I just don't think I'll be spendin' a lot of what I got left on the trail, that's all. Jesus, I ain't lookin' to die!"

"Well," Trevor said, "that's good to hear."

"Finish that beer," Flood said. "We got work to do."

Trevor made a face.

"It's too warm. We gotta get some cold beer."

Flood called the barman over.

"Any cold beer in town?"

"Sorry," the barman said, "not a drop."

Flood looked at Trevor, who frowned.

"Hey," the barman said, "are you Henry Flood?"

"I am," Flood said. "What's it to you?"

"Feller was in here earlier lookin' for you."

"Who's that?"

"Said his name was Clint Adams," the barman said. "That'd be the Gunsmith, right?"

"That's right," Flood said. "We're supposed to meet up. Where'd he say he'd be?"

"Said he'd be comin' back here later, and that you should meet him."

"See?" Flood said to Trevor. "He's here?"

"So what?" Trevor asked. "Still say he ain't no good on a drive."

"He went on his first drive when you was still in knee pants, boy," Flood said. "Lemme tell you, sometimes you need a good gun on a drive."

"Yeah, well, right now there's other things we need," Trevor said.

"You're right." Flood looked at the barman. "If Adams comes back in tell 'im to stay put and I'll find him here."

"Sure thing," the barman said.

"Let's go, Trevor."

As Flood and Trevor left the saloon they were being watched from across the street. The man watching was sitting in a wooden chair, his foot up on a post so he could rock back and forth on the rear legs. He was chewing on a toothpick, and as Flood and Trevor came out he stopped chewin' and rockin'.

He dropped his foot and leaned forward, squinting. He'd seen the two men go in, wasn't sure they were who he thought they were. But now he had a better look at them, and he knew.

The Flood outfit had made it to Doan's Crossing. The herd had to be somewhere outside of town. As Flood and Trevor split up and went separate ways, the man spit the toothpick out and stood up. He waited a minute, made up his mind, and then went in the same direction as Jack Trevor.

# FIVE

Halfway through his walk of Doan's Crossing, Clint decided it was just too depressing. He decided to head back to the saloon to await the arrival of Henry Flood. When he turned he saw Flood walking toward him. He decided to wait for the man to notice him, and Flood was almost in front of him before recognition dawned on his face.

"Clint!"

"I was wondering if you were going to walk right by me," Clint said.

"I'm sorry," Flood said, grabbing Clint's hand and pumping it enthusiastically. "I was thinkin' about somethin' else. When did you get to town?"

"Earlier today," Clint said. "I left a message for you at the saloon."

"I got it!" Flood said. "I just rode in with my ramrod, Jack Trevor."

"Trevor?" Clint asked. "The kid?"

"Not such a kid anymore, Clint," Flood said. "He's been my second for a while, now."

"As I recall he didn't like me very much," Clint said.

"Still doesn't," Flood laughed. "Listen, there's no place in Doan's Crossing to get a cold beer anymore?"

"That's what I heard."

"What about a decent cup of coffee?"

"Coffee, or trail coffee?"

"I like your trail coffee," Flood said, "but only on the trail, where it keeps me alert."

"Didn't there used to be a café—well, down here some place. Let's walk. We can get some coffee and something to eat."

"Suits me."

"What about Trevor?"

"He's got work to do," Flood said. "He can eat when he gets hungry."

They fell into step together and went looking for a café.

Roy Sobel grabbed Debra's legs and spread them while he drove himself in and out of her. It had been a long while since he'd fucked her, but it felt just like he remembered—damned fine! She was as hot as ever, inside and out. On the trail he often thought about her burning hot skin to keep him warm on cold nights.

Her pussy was so wet they were making wet sucking sounds as they strained against each other. He slid his hands from her calves so that he could grip her ankles and spread her even farther.

"You're gonna split me in half!" she complained.

"Shut up, bitch!" he snapped. "I'm payin', ain't I?"

He was paying, and he could do any damn thing he wanted with a whore he was paying for.

Debra could feel the strain in her thighs. If he spread her legs any farther she wouldn't be able to walk—or work—until those thigh muscles healed.

Roy was one of her more aggressive clients, but she made sure his aggression stopped short of actually hurting her. One time he had spread her so wide she thought her pussy was going to rip, and she had kicked him in the chin to get him off of her. He had come right back to her, mouth bloody but smiling, and finished what he'd started without hurting her. He was a dangerous man, because that violence was just barely controlled. When Roy came around Debra kept a knife under the pillow, just in case.

But she had to admit, he was more exciting than most of her clients. She never knew when she might have to cut him to get him off of her.

Clint and Flood found the café. Actually, they found *a* café, not at all sure it was the same one, but by then they were hungry.

They entered, found all of the six tables empty, and chose the one they wanted—in the back. A bald, sweaty man took their order, and started them out with a pot of coffee. They both ordered steaks, and the man went off to cook them— or burn then, judging from the smell that came from the kitchen a littler while later.

"Not as strong as yours," Flood said, when he tried the coffee. "Thank God."

"What's on your mind, Hank?" Clint asked. "Why'd you ask me to meet you here?"

Flood put his cup down and looked at Clint.

"I'm goin' on a drive, Clint. Maybe my last trail drive."

"That's too bad," Clint said. "What do you want me to do?"

"I want you to come with me."

"On a trail drive?" Clint shook his head. "I haven't been on one in years."

"Didja hear what I said?" Flood asked. "This might be not only my last trail drive, but *the* last trail drive."

"To tell you the truth," Clint said, "I thought the last trail drive had already happened."

"Not if I have anything to say about it," Flood said. "I got a thousand head, and I expect to pick up half that again between here and Montana."

"I remember when you drove three thousand head."

"Those days are gone," Flood said, glumly. "A thousand was all I could muster but, like I said, there's more out there roaming free."

"What about barbed wire?"

"We'll go around it," Flood said.

Portions of the famed trails—the Chisum, the Goodnight, and others—had since been blocked off by barbed wire. What was formerly open range was far from open, these days.

"How many men you got?" Clint asked.

"Ten," Flood said. "Some of my regulars. Enough to do the job, by far."

"With Trevor as your segundo?"

"That's right."

"He's not going to like this."

"Too bad."

"Why do you want me, Hank?"

"You ain't gonna like the answer."

"Try me."

"You're a legend," Flood said. "If this is my last—*the* last—trail drive, I want it to be remembered."

"When it comes to trail drives, Henry Flood is the legend, not me."

"Maybe with the two of us on this drive it'll be remembered."

"Hank . . . are you all right?"

"Whataya mean?"

"I mean is there something you're not telling me?" Clint asked. "You're not dying or something, are you?"

"We're all dyin', Clint," Flood said, "but me no sooner than you, I hope. Naw, I ain't dyin', I'm just gettin' old and tired. And like you said, the beeves ain't there to drive anymore. Not with folks shipping them by rail."

"So this is on the level?" Clint asked. "This 'last trail drive' business?"

"Of course it's on the level, Clint," Flood said. "Why would I lie to you?"

Clint gave his friend a long look.

"Okay, that time I really needed you as an extra man."

"You just about shanghaied me."

"Not this time," Flood said, as the waiter came with their steaming plates. "This time I'm askin'. Whataya say?"

# SIX

"You haven't changed," Debra said, pulling on her dressing gown.

Roy laughed. He was sitting on the edge of the bed, still naked, his penis flagging just a bit.

"I thought you was gonna kick me in the chin again," he said.

"I thought I was going to have to," she said. "You've got to learn there are certain ways a lady just doesn't bend."

"Don't mean I can't keep tryin'," he said.

"What brings you back to town after all this time?" she asked.

"Trail drive."

"I thought all the trail drives were done?"

"Not this one," he said.

"What makes this one so special?"

"The trail boss is Henry Flood."

She frowned.

"I know that name?"

"You should," Roy said. "He's as famous as Chisum and Goodnight."

"To you, maybe."

She lit a cigarette.

"We done?" she asked, blowing smoke.

He looked down at his dick, then back at her.

"I don't think so."

"Don't you have to be someplace?"

"I do," he said, "tomorrow mornin'."

"You aren't staying here with me until tomorrow morning," she said.

"I would," he said, "but I ain't got that much money. I only got enough for one more poke."

"Fine," she said. "Let me finish this cigarette. You just sit right there like you are, and I'll hop on."

"Sounds good."

"Stroke it a little for me," she said, "while I watch. Make it hard."

"Damn, woman!" he said. "Yer dirty."

"And isn't that why you come to see me?"

"It sure is." He took his cock in his hand and started stroking it. Before long it was standing long and hard—mostly because while she smoked with her right hand, she played with herself with her left, getting herself wet and ready.

"Okay," she said, stabbing out the cigarette, "here I come."

She dropped her robe, straddled his legs, reached down for his cock, and then sank down on it, taking it inside.

Hard for him to try to split her in half from here.

# SEVEN

Jack Trevor came out of the general store, stopped to light a quirley. He didn't see the man watching him from across the street.

He had purchased what they needed and made arrangements to have it all picked up by buckboard early the next morning. Now all he had to do was find a chuckwagon cook, and they didn't grow on trees. You couldn't just go into a restaurant or café and grab a cook out of the kitchen. Cooking out of a chuckwagon for a group of drovers was very different.

If he didn't find one, he and the other men were going to have to eat Henry Flood's cooking the whole way. That was not an option for him.

Clint and Flood finished their burned steaks. It was still better than what they had eaten lately on the trail. Even burned meat was better than beans day after day.

Over pie—peach for Clint, rhubarb for Flood—the trail boss asked, "Well? Ain't you given it enough thought, already?"

"I'm still thinking, Hank," Clint said. "You're asking me to give you three months of my life."

"You got other plans for that three months?"

"Well, no—"

"Can you think of a better way to spend them three months?"

"I can think of a lot of ways—"

"Okay, never mind that part," Flood said, waving his hands. "I know you'd rather sit at a poker table for three months."

"That's just one—"

"When's the last time you turned down a friend askin' for help?"

"The last time a friend asked me for three months—"

Flood sat back hard in his chair.

"Yer startin' to rile me!"

"Okay, take it easy," Clint said, laughing.

"Stop funnin' me like that, Clint," Flood said. "This is real important to me."

"I know it is, Hank," Clint said. "Look, I'll have to send some telegrams today. I was supposed to be someplace in about two months, but I can cancel."

"So you'll come?" Flood asked.

"As long as nobody else on the drive objects," Clint said.

"I'm the boss," Flood said. "Nobody's gonna say nothin' if I tell 'em—"

"Hold on," Clint said. "I've been on trail drives before where there was tension between some of the men. It doesn't make for a pleasant three months."

Flood scratched the beard stubble on his chin.

"I guess you're right," he said. "Well, I'll talk to the men. I don't think anybody's gonna say nothin' about it."

"What about Trevor?"

"I'll talk to Jack," Flood said. "I don't think I'll have a problem with him."

"Where is Trevor anyway?" Clint asked.

"He had to go and buy some supplies," Flood said. "And we gotta find us a cook. The one I had did a damn fool thing and now he can't come with us."

"What'd he do?" Clint asked.

"He died."

"Well," Clint said, "I might have somebody for you."

Clint and Flood entered the Crystal Saloon, found Jack Trevor standing at the bar nursing a warm beer. Clint could tell the man wasn't happy to see him.

"Adams," he said.

"Trevor."

"How'd you do, Jack?" Flood asked.

"I got the supplies," Trevor said, "we can pick 'em up in the mornin'. I'll have a couple of the men come in and collect 'em."

"What about a cook?"

"Well, now, there I didn't have much luck. In the old days we woulda found two or three of 'em sittin' around the saloon, waitin' to be asked."

"Well, Clint actually thinks there may be somebody in this saloon who can do the job?"

"Oh? That so? Is Adams an expert on chuckwagon cooks, now?"

"Not an expert," Clint said. "I just know there's somebody here who's done the job before."

"Who might that be, then?" Trevor asked.

Clint pointed a finger at the barman and said, "Him."

# EIGHT

"You say this fella's got experience?" Trevor asked.

"*I* don't say it," Clint said. "He said it earlier today when we were talking."

"Why were you and him talkin' about chuckwagons?" Trevor asked.

"We were just passing the time, Trevor," Clint said, "and he mentioned it."

"What's it matter why he said it?" Flood asked. "Let's find out who he's worked for, and maybe we'll get an idea if he's any good."

"I'll talk to him," Trevor said, turning to call the man over.

"Since I'm, here," Flood said, "I'll just listen in."

"Me, too," Clint said. When Trevor looked at him he added, "I've got nothing else to do."

"Suit yerself," Trevor said.

The barman saw them and came over.

"Nice to see ya back, Mr. Adams," he said. "Beer?"

"I've had enough warm beer for one day, Spud," Clint said. "Meet my friend, Jack Trevor and Henry Flood."

"Flood?" Spud's eyes popped.

"Spud Johnson, Hank," Clint said. "Used to be a chuckwagon cook."

"So he says," Trevor commented.

"Well, Mr. Johnson," Flood said, "who've you worked for?"

Johnson gave Flood a few names, and a few personality descriptions as well, enough to convince Flood that he was telling the truth.

"Well," Flood said, "sounds good enough for me."

"How do we know he can cook?" Trevor asked.

"No matter how he cooks," Flood said, "it has to be better than my cookin'."

"That's for sure," Clint said.

Trevor looked at both of them, then said to Flood, "It's up to you. You're the boss."

"Yeah, I am."

Trevor walked away, out the batwing doors.

"Spud, you're hired," Flood said. "Can you be ready to leave tomorrow?"

"Today, if you say so, Boss."

"Tomorrow will do," Flood said. "And Spud, on the trail you'll take your orders from me, and from Mr. Trevor."

"Yes, sir."

Flood looked at Clint.

"Now there's only you to make up your mind," Flood said.

"Yeah, I guess there is."


Jack Trevor stopped just outside the saloon, still didn't see the man across the street. He was mad—mad that Clint Adams would be coming along on the drive, even madder that Flood had hired the barman as their cook without consulting him. He was the segundo, he was supposed to have some say in who got hired and who didn't.

He decided to walk over to the livery and check on his horse. The animal was going to have to be sound for this trip. He had four others with the remuda back at the herd, but this one was his favorite.

As he headed for the livery stable the man watching him fell into step behind him.

Flood talked more with Spud Johnson, assuring him that the chuckwagon would be properly outfitted for the trip. Johnson then went to talk to the owner of the saloon to explain that he was leaving.

"After all," he said to Flood, "this was supposed to be a temporary job."

"The herd is just west of town, Spud," Flood said. "See you there early tomorrow."

"First light, Boss," Spud said. "I'll be there at first light."

Johnson came out from behind the bar to find the saloon owner.

"I better go and find Jack," Flood said. "He's the type to sulk and brood."

"He's mad that you hired Spud."

"He'll get over it."

"And he doesn't want me along."

"He'll get over that, too. He hired all the other men. He'll have to give me two. After all, I am the boss."

"I'll come with you to find him," Clint said. "In his mood he might be getting himself into trouble."

"Ah, if he gets into a fight he'll just be blowing off some steam, but come ahead."

Together, they left the saloon.

# NINE

They didn't find Jack Trevor until they reached the livery stable. At that point they'd pretty much been all over town.

"Why would he come here?" Clint asked. "He can't get into trouble here."

"Maybe not," Flood said, "but he might have wanted to check on his horse."

"I never knew a cowboy to put store in one horse. Not when he had a remuda to pick from?"

"Jack likes this particular horse for some reason. Well, you know all about havin' special feelings for a horse—first Duke, now this monster that you ride."

The livery seemed empty, except for the horses in the stalls. And the feet Clint saw sticking out of an empty stall.

"Hank!"

He hurried to the stall, followed by Flood. He leaned over the body and turned the man over.

"Is it—" Flood said.

"Yeah," Clint said, "Trevor. Somebody stabbed him in the back."

"Damn it, Jack!"

Clint stood up and stepped away so Flood could check for himself.

"Damn it, kid," Flood said, bowing his head.

"I'm sorry, Hank," Clint said. "I'll go and find the law after I take a look around and make sure whoever did this isn't still here."

"I can take care of that," Flood said. "Go find the sheriff, Clint."

"Any idea who might have done this?" Clint asked.

Flood stood up.

"Why would I?"

"You know Jack," Clint said. "He has a temper, right?"

"If he ran into somebody and got into a fight, how am I supposed to know who it was?"

"What if it was somebody following him," Clint asked. "Somebody who new him, and had a grudge."

"You mean one of my men?"

"Could be, right?"

"Could be anybody," Flood said. "How about that law?"

"I'll find him."

While Clint was gone Flood went through Jack Trevor's pockets. He'd given the man money to buy supplies. Whatever was left was rightfully his, but try explaining that to a lawman.

He looked around for Trevor's horse, found it standing in a storm, undisturbed. It also belonged to him.

That done, he returned to the body. He was saddened by the murder or Jack Trevor, but he had to act like a trail boss, too. Now he was not only going to have to replace a man, but his segundo, as well. And there were slim pickings in town.

He could only think of one man to replace him.

Clint found the sheriff's office, with the sheriff in it. The man was sitting at a rolltop desk that was set up flush against one wall.

"Help ya?" The sheriff was a sleepy-looking fifty, bloodshot, heavy-lidded eyes that indicated lack of sleep, or too much whiskey. Maybe both.

"There's been a murder."

"Where?"

"The livery."

The lawman stood up, grabbed his hat.

"Friend of yours?" he asked.

"More like a friend of a friend. We found him together."

"Good alibi," the sheriff said "for both of you."

"You're a suspicious man, Sheriff."

"Comes with the job."

They went out the door, headed for the stable.

"You got a name?" the lawman asked.

"Adams, Clint Adams."

"Adams . . . like the Gunsmith, Clint Adams?" the sheriff asked.

"That's right."

"How long you been in town?"

"Got here this morning," Clint said. "I meant to drop in on you, but never had the chance."

"Not even here a day and a dead man, already?"

"Oh, I had nothing to do with it," Clint said. "I just happened to find him."

"You mind tellin' me why you're in town?"

"To meet my friend."

"Your friend who is the friend of the dead man?"

"Now you've got it," Clint said.

"So, you're just a innocent bystander?"

"That's exactly what I am, Sheriff," Clint said. "An innocent bystander."

# TEN

When Clint and the sheriff got to the livery, Flood was standing there with another man.

"Pete," the sheriff said.

"Sheriff Lee."

"This fella says he found a dead body here," Pete said. He was a tall, string bean of a man in his sixties with skin that looked like old paper. "That right?"

"That's what this fella says, too," the lawman said. "This is Clint Adams. Pete owns the livery."

"And this is Henry Flood, Sheriff," Clint said.

"The trail boss," the sheriff said. "Nice to meet you. Sorry it's like this. Do you know this fella?"

"Yeah," Flood said. "He worked for me . . . and he was a friend of mine."

"What happened?"

"Looks like he was stabbed in the back," Flood said.

"Robbed?" the lawman asked.

"No, and he still has his gun in his holster."

The sheriff leaned over Trevor's body, confirmed what he had been told.

"His name's Jack Trevor," Flood said.

"Pete," the sheriff said, "go and get Doc Ryan."

"Sure, Sheriff."

The livery owner left. The sheriff stood to face Clint and Flood.

"What happened before this?" he asked. "Where did you last see Mr. Trevor?"

"The saloon," Flood said.

"What was goin' on at the saloon?"

"Nothin'," Flood said. "We were hirin' a cook for the trail drive."

"And you split up?"

"Jack wanted to check on his horse, I guess," Flood said. "Later we went lookin' for him."

"And found him here?"

"That's right, Flood said."

The sheriff looked at Clint. It wasn't exactly the story, but it was close enough.

"That's right, Sheriff," Clint said. "That's what happened."

"So somebody snuck up behind him and stabbed him," the sheriff said. "The question is why?"

"I don't know," Flood said.

"Did Mr. Trevor have any enemies?"

"Not in town," Flood said.

"Then where? In your camp?"

"That ain't what I meant," Flood said. "He didn't have any enemies that I know of."

Sheriff Lee looked back down at Trevor.

"I ain't no detective," he said. "There ain't much I can do about this other than have him taken to the undertaker's."

Clint was looking at the dirt floor of the stable, then looked at Flood.

"Hank, let me see your boots, Clint said."

"What?"

"The bottom of your boots."

Flood sat on a bale of hay and lifted both feet.

"Now you, Sheriff," Clint said.

THE LAST TRAIL DRIVE

The lawman lifted his one at the time, showing Clint the bottoms.

"Wait."

He knelt down, checked Trevor's boots.

"What is it, Clint?"

"There are some boot prints here, see 'em? The heel is scored in kind of a Z shape."

The sheriff and Flood took a look.

"If that print wasn't made by Pete, maybe it was made by the killer."

"If it wasn't made by somebody else puttin' up his horse," Flood said.

"Mr. Flood is right," the lawman said. "That ain't somethin' I could take to a judge."

"Well," Clint said, "we don't all have to justify ourselves to a judge. I'll check Pete's boots anyway, when he gets back."

Speak of the devil, Pete returned at that moment with a young man in tow. The man was carrying a black bag.

"Doctor Ryan?" Clint asked.

"That's right."

Ryan leaned down over Trevor's body.

"He's a little young," Flood said.

"He's real young," Sheriff Lee said, "but we need a doctor."

"Yup, he's dead," Ryan said.

"We knew that," Flood said sourly.

"Stabbed in the back by a wide blade," Ryan said, "by somebody who knows how to use a knife."

He stood up.

"I'll get some men to take him over to the undertaker's. There's not much else I can do."

"Not much more any of us can do," the lawman said.

"Pete, let me see your boots."

"Huh?"

# ELEVEN

Clint and Flood were back in the Crystal Saloon, sitting at a table near the back. There was a different man working as the barman. They had a beer in front of each of them, and a bottle of whiskey on the table with two glasses. Clint had taken one glass of whiskey just to have a drink with Flood for his deceased friend Trevor. Since then he'd been sipping his warm beer.

"I don't get it," Flood said. "Who'd wanna stick Trevor like that?"

"There must be something going on, Hank," Clint said. "This can't be a surprise. Trevor must have gotten somebody mad at him."

"Oh, he was a hothead. He had fights all the time, but they usually ended up with him and the other fella havin' a drink together."

"Not this time."

"No," Flood said. "Not this time." He poured himself a glass of whiskey.

Clint still thought something else had to be going on, but he didn't press it at that point.

"You've got a trail drive starting tomorrow, Hank," Clint warned.

"Yeah, yeah, one last drink to Jack's memory," Flood said. He tossed it down. "Now I gotta think about replacing him. I got my cook, but lost my segundo."

"You must have a man working for you who qualifies," Clint said.

"No, I don't," Flood said. "We hired experienced hands, but none of them knows anything about running a drive, handling men, handling *me*."

"Then you better start looking."

"I'm done looking," Flood said, looking across the table at Clint. "I want you."

"Look, Hank—"

"I was askin' you to come with me as a favor, Clint, and I woulda paid ya wages. Now I'll pay you to be my segundo."

"It's been years since I've been on a drive, Hank—" Clint started, but Flood cut him off.

"Clint, I need to replace Trevor with somebody the men will respect," he said. "I get that with you. In fact, they might even be afraid of you, which would also work."

"Hank, it isn't about the money—"

"I'll cut you in on the end," Flood said.

"I don't want your money."

"Then help, me, Clint," Flood said. "Help me. This is my last chance to feel alive again!"

Roy Sobel left the whorehouse feeling more than satisfied. It had been a memorable afternoon for him, which was what he wanted, because he didn't know if he was ever going to get back this way again. Not if—like Flood kept saying—this was going to be the last trail drive.

Sobel walked toward town, wondering what Andy Dirker had been doing for the past few hours. They had ridden into town together, and later today they'd be riding out to the herd. Dirker hadn't wanted a whore, so maybe he'd gone looking for a good saloon.

Sobel came across the Crystal, walked up to the bat-wings, and looked inside. He didn't see his friend. In fact, he didn't see much of anybody, but then his eyes fell on Henry Flood sitting at a table with another man. He decided not to go in. He didn't want to run into Flood in a saloon.

He backed away, thinking that the man with Flood wasn't Jack Trevor. Maybe Trevor hadn't come into town, but if he had that was somebody else Sobel didn't want to run into.

He continued his search for Andy Dirker, but kept to doorways and alleys so as not to run into a wandering Jack Trevor. He didn't know of many other saloons in town, but there were probably one or two. He'd check them out, and if he could find Dirker he'd just ride out to the herd on his own.

"What's your crew like?" Clint asked.

"Good men—experienced," Flood said. "I didn't want any beginners on this drive. Didn't wanna have to look after anybody."

"There probably aren't that many youngsters around looking to go on a trail drive anyway," Clint said.

"You got that right. There ain't nobody on my crew under thirty-five."

"Okay, Hank."

"Okay?" Flood asked. "You'll do it?"

"I'll do it," Clint said. "Not for wages and not for a piece. I'll just do it for you."

"Jesus, Clint, I appreciate it."

"Yeah, yeah," Clint said. "I'll ride out to your camp in the morning."

"I'll have a couple of men comin' in with a buckboard for supplies."

"That's a fine," Clint said. "I might pass them on the way."

"I'll ride back tonight and let everybody know what happened," Flood said.

"I think I'll get a bath while I have the chance. Might be a long time before I get another one."

Flood picked up the whiskey bottle. "How about a drink on it?"

If the beer had been cold he would have turned it down. Instead he said, "Why not? One more—for both of us!"

# TWELVE

Roy Sobel found Andy Dirker sitting in a wooden chair in front of the hardware store. He was rocking back and forth on the rear legs, chewing on a toothpick.

"You finished with your whore?" Dirker asked as Sobel approached.

"Yup," Sobel said. "I'm ready to go on the drive." There was no other chair, so he sat down on the edge of the board-walk. "What've you been doin'?"

"Nothin'," Dirker said. "Just sittin' here."

"You ate?"

"Not yet."

"Let's go get a steak, then, before we go back to camp."

"Suits me," Dirker said.

They got up and started walking.

"Saw Flood in the Crystal," Sobel said, "but not Trevor. We don't wanna run into either of them. We're supposed to already be in camp."

"Don't think we have to worry about that," Dirker said. "I heard they had some trouble."

"What kind of trouble?"

"I heard somethin' happened to Trevor."

"Like what?"

Dirker shrugged.

"Don't rightly know," he said. "Just heard there was some trouble."

"Well then, maybe we'll have a chance to get back to camp before they notice we're gone."

"Right now, I'm just thinkin' about that steak," Dirker said.

"Me, too."

Debra decided that Roy Sobel was her last john for the day. She was going to go and have a hot bath and a meal, and then go to her place at the rooming house.

She was the only whore who didn't actually live in the same room where she worked. She'd spent too many years doing that, and she had saved enough money over the years to get her own place.

As she passed through the front hall in her street clothes she heard from two of the girls.

"The princess is leaving," one of them said.

"Yeah, she's too good to live here with us," the other girl said. "Goin' to her rooming house."

Debra ignored them, and as she went out the door she heard one of them mutter, "Wish I could afford a rooming house."

"Shhh," the other one said.

Debra smiled and closed the door behind her.

Clint went to the barber shop, which had bathtubs in the back rooms behind it. He paid for a bath, waited while the man brought buckets of hot water and filled the tub. He turned down the offer of a haircut and shave, ushered the man out of the room and then undressed and sank gratefully into the tub of hot water.

In the room next door to his, Debra was sitting in her bath-tub, wondering if Eddie the barber was peeking in at her through a hole in the wall. His wife wouldn't let him come to the whorehouse, and she'd caught him peeking once before. She told him if she ever caught him again she'd poke his eyes out, and then he'd have to explain that to his wife.

She luxuriated in the hot water, used a cloth and soap to clean any vestige of her clients from her body. The hot water felt good on her right thigh, where Roy Sobel may, indeed, have caused her to stretch a muscle.

She was lying back, enjoying the last of the heat before the water began to cool, when she heard something bang against the wall on her left.

She sprang up out of the tub, grabbed a towel, wrapped it around her, and went to catch Eddie peeking at her.

Clint's tub was close to the wall, so when he picked his gun belt up off the seat of the chair next to him and went to hang it on the back, the gun swung and banged into the wall before it settled into position, hanging from the back of the chair, within easy reach.

# THIRTEEN

As the door to the room slammed open Clint's hand streaked for his gun. He found himself pointing it at a blond woman standing in the doorway with a towel wrapped around her.

She froze when she saw the gun pointing at her.

"Wha—" she said.

"That's what I want to know," Clint said. He holstered the gun. "What's going on?"

"I—I was taking a bath in the room next door, when I heard something hit the wall. I thought Eddie—the barber—I thought he was back here trying to peek in at me again. He, uh, he done it last time."

"I see," Clint said. "Well, I think when I hung my gun on the back of the chair it banged into the wall. I'm sorry it caused you to get out of your tub."

"Oh, uh, it's okay, I guess, but—"

"Why don't you go back and finish your bath?" Clint suggested.

"Well, I would, but by now the water's probably gone cold."

She looked at the steam that was still rising in Clint's tub.

Suddenly, he recognized her as the woman who had been smoking on the balcony of the whorehouse.

"Well, my water is still pretty hot."

"I see that."

"I'd invite you to get in with me," he said,. "but . . ."

"But what?"

"I saw you out on the balcony before, smoking," he said.

"Oh, was that you?"

"That was the whorehouse, right."

"Right," she said. "What's wrong, you don't like whores?"

"I think whores are beautiful," he said. "I think you're beautiful—"

"Thanks . . ."

"—but I make it a practice not to pay for sex."

"Really?" She was fascinated, regarded him with sudden interest. "You've never paid for a woman?"

"Never."

"I find that hard to believe," she said. "Why is that?"

"I just never got into the habit," he said. "Besides, there are plenty of women out there."

"I see," she said. "Well, I guess you're in luck, then."

"Why's that?"

"I happen to be finished for the day," she said. "That's why I was having a bath."

"Well," he said, "what do we do, then?"

"Why don't I feel your water and see if it's hot enough for the both of us?"

"Sure."

She approached the tub, knelt down beside it, and put her hand in. The towel was wrapped tightly around her, but he could see from her rounded shoulders and thighs that she was a woman with some meat on her.

She dipped her hand in, sloshed the water around, and then pushed her hand down between his legs. She found his penis, felt it begin to swell in her hand. Oddly—given her profession—she found herself growing excited. Sex with a man who wasn't paying was not a common occurrence for her.

"Wow, it is very hot," she said, stroking his cock.

"Better make up your mind before it cools off," he said.

"Oh," she said, "I've made up my mind."

"Better close the door, then."

She got to her feet, walked to the door, closed it, then turned and let the towel drop to the floor. Her breasts were pale, almost pear-shaped, with pink nipples. Her belly was nicely rounded, with a deep belly button. Between her legs was a heavy tangle of hair that was more golden than the hair on her head.

"Well?" she asked. "Do you approve?"

"Oh, yes, ma'am," he said. "I approve very much."

"Enough to pay?" she asked.

"Well, now," he said, "I guess if I was ever going to pay for a whore it'd be you, here and now."

"So, should we talk price?"

"Do you want to?"

"Hell, no," she said. "Right now I'm randier than I can ever remember being, and I think it's because you don't wanna pay."

"If that's the case," he said, "then get your beautiful, big ass in this tub!"

# FOURTEEN

Luckily, Eddie believed in supplying large bathtubs for his clientele.

Debra approached the bathtub and bent to step in, her full breasts swaying with the movement. The pink nipples had already extended themselves impressively, and Clint was reaching for them as she stepped in and sank down into the water. He leaned forward, cupped her breasts in his hands, holding their weight gently, thumbing the distended nipples.

"Mmm," she said, as he squeezed both breasts. She reached between his legs, took his hard cock in both hands, stroking it lovingly. Clint thought that if Eddie really did peek into these rooms he was getting more than he ever bargained for now.

She scooched forward, sliding her legs atop his, and on either side of him, so that they were able to get very close to each other. Clint pulled her close and kissed her. Debra, who did not ever kiss her clients, melted into the kiss and groaned into his mouth.

"Jesus," she said breathlessly.

"Yeah."

"I mean, Jesus, I'm a goddamned whore," she said. "I'm not supposed to feel . . . feel like this."

"You were a woman before you were a whore," he told her.

"I haven't been a woman in a long time," she said. "A very, very long time."

He pulled her close, crushed her wet breasts against his chest, and said into her ear, "You sure feel like a woman to me."

She leaned into him then, abruptly pushed away, and got to her feet, almost upsetting the tub and splashing water all over the floor.

"What is it?" he asked.

She got out of the tub, almost slipped and fell, but righted herself.

"Not here," she said, "not here, not like this."

She stood there then, as if confused.

"What's your name?"

"Huh? Oh, Debra. My name's Debra."

"Debra, do you want to go someplace else?"

"Someplace?"

"Like my room?" he asked. "At the hotel?"

"I don't—I don't know what to do."

He got up, stepped out of the tub and went to her, taking her by the shoulders.

"I have to leave town tomorrow," he said. "If that helps. I don't know if I'll ever be coming back."

"That doesn't help a lot," she said. "I'm real confused here. W-what's your name?"

"Clint Adams."

"That means somethin'—wait, wait. The Gunsmith?" she asked.

"That's right."

"Oh, wow," she said, "I didn't know . . ."

"Look," he said, "why don't we get dried off, go someplace and talk. Maybe that's all you need is to talk about . . . something?"

"Mr. Adams—"

"Clint, please," he said. "After all." He gestured to the fact that they were both naked.

"Clint . . . I really don't need to talk," she said. "But I do need to get out of here."

"Okay," he said. "I have a few towels. Your clothes?"

"Next door."

"Okay," he said, again. "Let's get dressed."

"And?"

"We'll cross that bridge when we come to it."

Debra rushed back to her own room, where she'd left her clothing. She dried off and got dressed. Her breathing had not returned to normal.

This was amazing, she thought. She hadn't been stirred by a man that way in . . . well, years, or maybe even . . . ever.

What the hell was going on?

Clint dried off and got dressed, strapped on his gun. He knew that something had happened earlier, when he and Debra had seen each other—he from the ground, and she from the balcony. Now, being this close to her, he knew it was special.

But special wasn't something a whore was used to, and she was confused. But since he was leaving town with Flood's outfit in the morning, if he was going to help her through it, it had to be tonight . . . now.

And if all she needed to do was talk—although she didn't seem to think that was what she needed—he could do that for her, too.

# FIFTEEN

"Mr. Flood?"

Flood looked up from his seat in the saloon. Since Clint left he had slowly worked on the bottle until it was almost gone. He frowned now, trying to see who was standing over him.

"What? Who's that?"

"Spud, sir," Spud Johnson said. "Are you all right?"

"Me? Sure, sure, I'm fine, just fine," Flood said. "Spud, did you say?"

"Yes, sir," Spud said. "You hired me to be the cook."

"Right, right," Flood said. "I, um, remember that." Although he wasn't really sure he did.

"Mr. Flood, can I help you get back to camp?" Spud asked.

"Um, yeah, that would be . . . um, good . . . Do you have a horse?"

"Uh, no, sir."

"Well, that's okay," Flood said. "I got one for you. Used to belong to a friend of mine. His name was Jack Trevor. Did you know Jack?"

"No, sir, I didn't."

"Well, actually," Flood said, "the horse belongs to me. Jack was just ridin' it. Okay, come on."

Flood got to his feet, swayed, and would have fallen if Spud hadn't grabbed him.

"Whoa!" he said.

"I gotcha, sir."

"Yeah, you do," Flood said. "Now, why don't you walk us over to the livery, and we'll get us those horses. You can come out to the camp and check out your chuck wagon. How's that sound?"

"It sounds good, Boss, but . . . can you ride?"

"Sure, I can ride," Flood said. "And the fresh air will do me some good, don't ya think?"

"Yessir, I do think."

"Then let's go, Spud," Flood said. "Let's go."

Clint and Debra left the barber shop and stopped just outside.

"I'm sorry," she said. "I didn't mean to act like some spooked virgin."

"You didn't."

She laughed.

"Yeah, I did. Truth was, I didn't know what I was supposed to do with what I was feeling. I mean, I've been a whore a long time. I thought I was pretty much dead inside."

"I don't think that's true," he said. "Let's walk."

She didn't argue, and even allowed him to pick the direction. He headed them off toward his hotel.

"I don't live in the whorehouse," she said. "I've got a room in the boarding house. Everybody thinks that's strange. Do you think that's strange?"

"No, I don't."

"Why not?"

"How many other people do you know who live where they work?"

She laughed again, this time with more humor than irony.

"That's right, isn't it?"

"Yup, it is."

Clint looked ahead and saw the sheriff coming toward them.

"Debra, you got any problem with talking to the sheriff?"

"No," she said, "but he's got problems talking to me—or any woman, for that matter."

"That's so?"

"He just sort of blathers on. Doesn't have the first idea how to talk to a woman. You know him?"

"Just met him today."

"You watch. He'll stare at me, but talk to you."

As the lawman reached them, Clint saw him lick his lips, take a quick look at Debra, and then fix his eyes on Clint.

"Sheriff, can I help you?"

"Uh, well, I just wanted to let you know the, uh, doctor didn't find anything else unusual about the body of poor Mr. Trevor."

"I didn't think he would," Clint said. "Seems like a pretty straight forward murder."

"Yes, it does. Have you seen Mr. Flood?"

"Not for a couple of hours. Why?"

"I wanted to see what he wanted done about a funeral," the lawman said.

"I don't think that'll be necessary," Clint said. "Trevor didn't have any family or friends in town."

"But he had men who worked for him, right?"

"I don't think they'd be coming into town for a funeral."

"Probably not. Well, then, there's still the matter of a coffin, and a grave . . ."

Clint took out some money and pushed it into the sheriff's hands.

"Would you see that the undertaker gets that?" he asked. "I think it should take care of everything."

The sheriff didn't look at the money in his hands.

"I'm sure it will," he said. "Thank you. Will you be, uh, leaving town?"

"First thing in the morning, Sheriff," Clint said. "You won't have to worry about me being in town after today."

"Well," the man said, "it's not that I was worried so much as . . . you know, concerned."

"I understand. Well, good-bye, Sheriff."

"Good-bye," the lawman said, then suddenly looked at Debra. "Ma'am."

"Sheriff."

He turned and crossed the street with a quickening pace.

"That's the first time he ever looked at me like I was a person," she said. "You think that was because I'm with you?"

"Maybe," Clint said.

"What's this about a murder?"

"Why don't you come up to my room, and I'll tell you all about it?"

"Sure," she said. "Why not?"

# SIXTEEN

Spud walked Henry Flood over to the livery, where he allowed his new boss to sit on a bale of hay while he saddled both horses, Flood's and the one that used to belong to Jack Trevor.

"Were these Trevor's?" he asked, showing Flood two saddlebags.

"Yeah, I guess," Flood said. "Let's take 'em back to the camp, and I'll have a look tomorrow."

"What about buryin' him?" Trevor asked.

Flood wiped his face with both hands and, for a moment, Spud didn't think the man had heard him.

"I'll come back tomorrow mornin' and arrange it," he said, wearily.

Trevor doubted that. Flood was drunk and exhausted. Spud just hoped this trail drive was going to get going on time.

Maybe, he thought, if he gave his boss a good breakfast it would improve his mood.

"Okay, Boss," he said, grabbing Flood's arm, "let's get you in the saddle."

Debra Moore was something she had never been before, and never thought she would be, especially in a man's room.

She was a nervous whore.

"Have a seat," Clint said.

There were no chairs in the room so she sat at the foot of the bed. For the moment, Clint remained standing.

"I don't have anything to offer you," he said, apologetically. "To drink, I mean."

"That's okay," she said. "I was just going to have a bath and then go to bed."

She blushed suddenly and thought, What the hell is wrong with me?

"Debra, do you want to talk?"

"No."

"What would you like to do?

"Truthfully?" she asked. "I'd just like to get our clothes off and have sex. Usually, I fuck for money. It's been a long time since I just had sex with a man."

"Well," he said, "I guess we could do that . . ."

"You didn't seem so hesitant in the bath house."

"I'm not hesitant," Clint said. "I just don't want you to do anything you're gonna regret tomorrow."

"What's it matter to you?" she asked. "You're going to be gone tomorrow."

"Good point."

She stood up. She was wearing a men's shirt that was too large for her, a pair of trousers, and a pair of boots. When she walked the street she didn't like to show herself off. Men stared, and women glared, and she didn't need any of that. She got enough of it when she was at work.

She unbuttoned her shirt, peeled it off, and then sat down to remove her boots before sliding her trousers off. Clint did his best not to watch as he removed his own clothes. But he couldn't help catching a glimpse of her from time to time, and by the time he was naked, he was also fully erect. When she finished and looked at him her eyes locked on his hard cock.

"Wow," she said, "there's somethin' I didn't get to see in the bath."

"You had a hold of it, though," he said.

"Yeah, but . . . look at it. That's about the prettiest cock I've ever seen . . . and believe me, I've seen my share."

# SEVENTEEN

There was still some awkwardness between them, even while they were naked. But once Clint took Debra into his arms, and their hot bodies pressed together, all their reservations seemed to fade away.

She came alive against him, rubbing herself all over him, reaching for his cock, taking it in both hands and then dropping to her knees.

"Damn," she murmured, "so pretty . . ."

She stroked it, took his testicles in one hand, then licked the fingers of her right hand and used it to wet the head of his penis. Her tongue came out, then, and wet it some more. She was going slowly, because this was something she only did for men when they asked for it, and then with no enthusiasm. Most of them came to her smelling like the trail, and when they removed their pants the odor got even worse. But they expected her to gobble their smelly cocks with pleasure.

Clint's cock was clean, and she was sure it wasn't just because he had just come from a bath. He struck her as a man who kept himself clean, even on the trail. And if he came off the trail and was going to see a woman, she was sure he'd clean himself up first.

He was simply like no man she'd ever met or been with before.

Clint filled his hands with Debra's breasts, enjoying the feel of them—smooth skin, but heavy and solid in his palms. He lifted her to her feet, turned her, and deposited her onto the bed. For a moment she was afraid he was just going to spread her legs and thrust himself in. Instead, he lowered himself onto the bed with her and lovingly began to kiss her body—her breasts, her nipples, her belly, down and down until he was nestled between her legs, his face pressed into that golden bush, tongue seeking her out.

When his tongue touched her she jumped. As a whore, no man had ever seen to her pleasure—and certainly not before his own.

His tongue lapped at her, made her wet and sensitive, while his hands moved up and cupped her breasts again, pinching her nipples. The combination of sensations drove her over the edge to her first orgasm in years.

But not the first of the night.


"Who's there?" someone yelled.

"Take it easy," Spud said. "My name's Spud Johnson. I'm the new cook."

"Who's that with you?"

"Your boss, Mr. Flood."

A man with a rifle stepped out into the open from behind a stand of junipers.

"What's wrong with him?"

"Drunk."

The man peered at Spud suspiciously.

"How do I know he hired you?"

"Wake him up and ask him," Spud suggested.

"Where's Jack?"

"Well, that's kinda why Mr. Flood is drunk," Spud said.

Suddenly, the man stepped back and pointed his rifle at Spud.

"Ain't that Jack Trevor's horse yer ridin'?" he demanded.

"Hold on, hold on," Spud said. "Yeah, it was Trevor's horse, but he's dead."

"What?"

"Somebody killed him."

"Who?"

"I don't know."

The man with the rifle looked at Henry Flood again.

"Is Mr. Flood alive?"

"Yeah, he's alive," Spud said. "I told you, he's drunk."

"And was he drunk when he hired you?"

"No," Spud said. "He got drunk after Trevor was killed."

"How was Jack killed?"

"Somebody stabbed him in the back."

"Jeez!"

Spud sniffed the air.

"Somethin's burnin'," he said.

"Yeah, one of the boys decided to try to make somethin' ta eat."

"Doesn't smell like he's doin' a very good job," Spud said.

"Yeah, well, the boys are hungry."

"Well, I can fix somethin'," Spud said, "but maybe you wanna make sure Mr. Flood is alive first?"

The man studied on that for a minute, then put up his rifle.

"Hell, no," he said. "If you can cook, then get to it!"

# EIGHTEEN

Debra Moore was lying across the bed, still naked, in a daze. Her pale, smooth skin was dappled with perspiration, her golden hair a wild, exotic tangle around her head.

"Oh my God," she said.

"I'll take that as a compliment," Clint said.

"That's how I mean it, believe me," she said. "I'm used to having men grunt and groan on me, and then roll off when they're done. I've never had anybody spend that much time on me, making sure that I was satisfied."

"Then you spend too much time at work," Clint told her. "You need to spend more time with men on your own."

"Not the men in this town," she said. "Not the men I've had to deal with over the past ten years or so. Are you like this because you're a legend? Does that have anything to do with it?"

"I'm like this because I like being with women," he said, "and I want them to like being with me."

"Well, oh my God!" she said. "Have you ever been with a woman who didn't like it?"

"I'm sure I have," he said, although he couldn't remember anyone in particular.

"I can't imagine that," she said, lifting her head to look

at him. Her eyes fell on his penis, which was still hard. "I have to take care of that."

"It's okay—"

"No, no," she said, rolling over and leaning over him. "I mean I have to—as in if I don't I'll die."

"Well, in that case," he said, "be my guest."

The simplest and fastest thing Spud could think to make was some chunky chili. The meat, chicken, peppers, and onions just went into one pot with olive oil, simmered there until he added the seasoning, beans, and tomatoes. While it was cooking he made some corn bread and some tortillas so the men would have a choice.

By the time Henry Flood was up and walking around the men were sitting with their bowls full of chili, happily eating and dipping with their bread.

"What the hell—" he said.

"Supper's on, Boss," one of the hands said. "That new cook you hired is the best."

Flood walked over to the chuckwagon, stared at Spud.

"Spud Johnson, Boss," Spud said, "Remember?"

"Yeah . . . Oh, yeah, I remember. What you got there, Spud?"

"Just some quick chili I threw together. Want a bowl, Boss?"

"I feel like hell, but I sure do."

"Corn bread or tortillas with it?"

"Can I get both?"

"You're the boss."

Spud handed Flood a bowl of chili, a hunk of corn bread, and a rolled up tortilla. Flood went to sit with the men and eat.

"Is somebody on watch?" he asked.

"Henderson is, Boss," Eddie Mott said.

"Bring him a bowl of chili when you get a chance, Eddie," Flood said.

"Sure, Boss."

"Hey, Mr. Flood?" Dan Quick said.

"Yeah?"

"Henderson said that cook tol' him Jack Trevor was dead. That true?"

"Yeah, it's true," Flood said. "Somebody stabbed him in the back."

"Did they catch who did it?"

"No," Flood said, sourly. "That's why I said 'somebody' did it."

"So what are we doin' then?" someone asked. "We still pullin' out tomorrow?"

"We are," Flood said. "I need two men to go to town at first light and get our supplies from the general store."

Two men volunteered. Well, seven men volunteered, but Flood pointed out two he figured would not try to get the saloon to open for them.

"What about Jack?" Eddie asked.

"What about him?"

"Well, he was segundo," Eddie said. "Who's gonna replace him?"

"I got a replacement already," Flood said. "He'll be here tomorrow mornin'."

The men all exchanged glances. Obviously they'd expected a replacement to be picked from their number.

"Who is it?" Eddie asked.

"You'll find out in the mornin'," Flood said, brushing him off. "Okay, listen up, here's who I want on night duty . . ."

Sitting at the back of the group of men eating chili were Roy Sobel and his friend, Andy Dirker. They had managed to get back to camp before Flood returned.

"Wonder who the new segundo's gonna be?" Sobel said, around a mouthful of chili.

Dirker remained silent, but he thought he knew.

# NINETEEN

Debra could not recall ever treating another man's penis the way she was treating Clint's—lovingly.

She positioned herself between his legs, stroked him until he was painfully hard, then took him deeply into her mouth and began to ride him wetly. He groaned, began moving his hips in unison with her head.

She rubbed her hands over his thighs, belly and chest while she continued to suck him. She was such an expert that she used no hands. She was able to take him to the brink, then back him off, then to the brink again, only using her mouth and tongue and throat.

She made an "Mmmmm" sound at one point, and he didn't know if it was because she was enjoying herself, or because she wanted him to feel the vibrations from the humming, which he did feel, right down to his toes.

"Jesus, Debra—" he said.

"No, not yet," she said, although she did release him from her mouth. She straddled him, smiled down at him and said, "First I want a ride."

"Fine with me," he said, reaching for her . . .

\* \* \*

Flood walked over to where Spud was cleaning up after everyone had finished eating.

"Well, looks like you can cook," Flood said.

"Yessir," Spud said. "I'm glad they all liked it."

"Listen . . . thanks for gettin' me back to camp."

"Sure, Boss."

"Now that I've had a small nap and a meal, I'm feelin' a lot better."

"That's good."

"Except about Jack Trevor."

"Oh, yeah," Spud said, "I'm real sorry about that."

"Say, you didn't notice anything in the saloon, did ya?" Flood asked. "I mean, anybody hangin' around, maybe followin' us?"

"I'm real sorry, Mr. Flood, but I didn't see nobody," Spud said.

"That's okay, Spud," Flood said. "Good job on the chili."

"I'm figurin' on makin' a mess of eggs and bacon for breakfast, Boss, with some biscuits."

"You go ahead and make whatever you want, Spud," Flood said. "You got all the supplies you'll be needin' in your wagon?"

"I took a quick look, but yeah, it seems well stocked."

"Good, good. I'm gonna ride out and take a look at the herd with a few of the men. I'll see you later—or in the mornin'."

"Okay, Boss."

Flood walked away. Spud was thankful he'd gotten through the day without getting shot by the sentry, and he seemed pretty secure in his new job—at least, for the next three months or so.

When Clint flipped Debra over onto her hands and knees, she cooperated fully, and happily. This was nothing like the sex she'd been having in grubby whorehouse rooms for years.

This was the kind of sex that was going to have her questioning her profession after it was over.

But as Clint gripped her wide hips and slid his penis up into her wet pussy from behind she didn't want it to end—ever. She had no idea what time it was, or what day it was.

And she didn't care.

Clint couldn't remember having been with a woman who enjoyed sex so much. And given Debra's job it was amazing to him that she was acting like a woman who had just discovered sex—except she was very, very good at it.

She had ridden him for a long time, her breasts mesmerizing him as they swayed in his face. He was able to stay with her, but it took every effort he had not to just explode.

Once she climbed off him, he gave in to the urge to flip her over and take her from behind, and she didn't mind at all.

He drove himself into her, and at the same time she rocked back into him. As their efforts continued, they both became covered by a sweaty sheen, and his hands began to slip on her hips. She grunted with every thrust, and in between grunts he thought she was laughing. She had a body made for sex, and he was pleased to enjoy it, but he doubted he was enjoying it as much as she was.

Maybe she was enjoying it for the first time in years—maybe in her life. Idly, he wondered if she'd want to talk when they were finished—but then all thoughts fled as he felt his orgasm building, and from then on he concentrated only on pursuing that.

# TWENTY

"Well, this is just fine," Debra said.

"What is?" Clint asked.

"You've ruined me," she said. "How can I go back to being a whore after this?"

"I didn't mean to cause you a career change," he said. "Should I apologize?"

"Hell, no!"

They were lying side by side, catching their breath.

"So do something else with your life," he suggested.

"Like what?" she asked. "At my age how can I change?"

"You're not that old."

"If I'm not an old whore," she said, "then I'm an old maid."

"At . . . what? Thirty?"

"Thirty-two."

"Oh, yeah, that's real old."

"It is, for an unmarried woman."

"There are lots of jobs you could get, Debra," he said.

"That may be true," she said, "but not in this town. I'd have to leave here and start over again."

"You seem to me to be the kind of woman who would have some money saved."

"What makes you say that?"

"Well, for one thing you have your own room, away from the whorehouse. You have to be able to pay for that, somehow."

"Well, you happen to be right," she said. "I do have some money put away."

"There you go," he said. "Buy a stagecoach ticket and get out of this town."

"And go where?"

"Anywhere," he said. "What's it matter?"

"And wherever I go, will I find another man like you?" she asked.

"You'll probably find more than one," he said. "You'll have to beat them off with a stick and make a choice."

"Yeah, right."

He turned his head to look at her. She sensed it and turned hers to look at him.

"You'll never know unless you try," he said.

"Well," she said, "I can't very well argue with that, can I?"

They got dressed and Debra took Clint to a small café where they wouldn't be stared at.

"You know," she said, "the legend and the whore?"

"Men stare at you because you're beautiful," he said, as they sat.

"Women glare at me for the same reason," she said.

"They should keep their husbands at home."

"Well, here I'm just Debbie. The waitress and her husband run this place."

He looked around at the other empty tables.

"Doesn't look like they do a booming business." And it wasn't just due to the late hour.

"Nobody does, these days. I'm sure you've noticed Doan's Crossing is dying."

"All the more reason for you to leave."

A waitress came out of the kitchen, saw them, and came over, smiling. She'd been pretty once, but that had been before life had gotten so hard. She looked beaten down, tired, and ten years older than she was, which was probably forty.

"Hey, Debbie, who's your friend?" the woman asked.

"Annie, this is Clint Adams. Clint, this is Annie Campbell. Her husband, Charlie, is the cook."

"Best cook in town," Annie said.

"I hope so," he said. "I had a horrible steak this afternoon.

"Well, we can fix that. Steak?"

"Please."

"Just a bowl of stew for me, Annie. A small one—it's late."

"I know," Annie said. "I'm going to lock the door. Normally, we'd be closed, but for you . . ."

"Could I bother you for a cup of coffee?" Clint asked.

Annie smiled at him and said, "How about a whole pot?"

He grinned back and said, "I think I love you."

"I never asked you why you have to get going early in the morning?" Debra said.

"I'm riding with a trail drive."

"The Henry Flood drive?" she asked.

"That's right. You know Flood?"

"No," she said, "but I know one of the hands, Roy Sobel."

"Customer of yours?"

"Used to be a regular customer. Hadn't seen him for years until recently."

"Good drover?" Clint asked.

"I don't know that about him," she said. "I know that he has a tendency to be . . . violent. I always kept a knife under my pillow when I was with him."

"Violent, huh?"

"Well, around women," she said. "I don't think he was violent around men. In fact, I get the feeling he's pretty easily led. Probably why he's so aggressive with women."

"Do you analyze all your customers that way?" he asked.

"A whore better be able to size up her john pretty quick—if she wants to stay alive."

After a wonderful steak and a great pot of coffee, Clint walked Debra to her rooming house. They stopped right out front.

"Sure I can't spend the night in your room?" she asked.

"I have to get going real early, Debra," he said. "If you spend the night, I'll get no sleep at all."

"And no chance you'll be back this way?"

"What's the difference?" Clint asked. "You'll be gone by then."

# TWENTY-ONE

When Clint got to the street the next morning, saddlebags over his shoulder, rifle in hand, he saw the buckboard at the general store with two men loading supplies. He walked over and was standing by the buckboard when they came out with sacks on their shoulders.

"Need some help?" he asked.

The two men dumped their sacks into the half-loaded buckboard and turned to face him.

"Who are you?" one asked

"Name's Clint Adams."

"You're the new segundo," the other one said.

"Yes."

"And the Gunsmith," the first man said.

"That's right."

"My name's Daltry," the first man said, extending his hand.

"I'm Roland."

Clint shook hands with both men.

"And we can use all the help we can get."

Clint put his rifle and saddlebags on the buckboard.

"Let's get to it."

\* \* \*

Once the buckboard was loaded, Clint told them to go on ahead.

"I'll saddle my horse and be along."

"Okay, Boss," Daltry said.

"Thanks for the help," Roland said.

Clint nodded, picked up his saddlebags and rifle again. The two men climbed up on to the buckboard and headed out of town. Clint went to the livery to saddle Eclipse.

When he caught up to the two men, they looked at him in surprise.

"You caught up quick," Daltry said.

"Yeah, but look what he's ridin'," Roland commented.

"That's some horse," Daltry said.

"Yeah, he is," Clint replied. "Come on, let's pick it up. Flood wants to get moving today."

"That's why he got us movin' this mornin' even before sunup," Daltry said.

"Well then, let's keep moving," Clint said.

When they rode into camp, Flood greeted Clint and had two men take the buckboard from Daltry and Roland, so they could eat breakfast.

"Come on over to the fire," Flood said. "I'll have somebody take care of your horse."

"Just leave him be," Clint said. "We're going to be moving out soon anyway, right?"

"That's right."

"Just have somebody give him some grain, but don't try to touch him," Clint said. "They'll lose their fingers."

"Right. I'll meet you by the fire."

Flood went to find somebody who could follow Clint's instructions and feed Eclipse.

As Clint approached the fire in front of the chuckwagon, Spud stepped up and handed him a plate of scrambled eggs and a cup of coffee. Clint tasted the coffee right away and nodded approvingly.

"Now that's what I call trail coffee," he said. "What's in the eggs?"

"Peppers, onions, some crumbled bacon," Spud said.

"Sounds good." He forked some in. "Tastes great. Thanks, Spud."

"No, man, thank you," Spud said. "Because of you I got a reason to live again."

"For three months, anyway," Clint said, sitting on a crate.

"Well, yeah," Spud said, "but who's to say this really is the last trail drive, ya know? Things could change."

"I guess they could," Clint said, but he didn't think it was very likely.

Flood came back, got a cup of coffee from Spud, and sat next to Clint.

"After you finish your breakfast I'll introduce you to all the men," he said. "They're all good boys."

"Maybe not."

"Whataya mean?"

"I mean, for all we know Trevor's killer is one of these men," Clint said. "What better way to slip out of town than as part of this crew?"

"I know these boys, Clint," Flood said.

"All of them?"

"Well . . . most of 'em."

"Really?" Clint asked. "Why don't you tell me about the ones you don't know so well?"

# TWENTY-TWO

As it turned out Flood was dead sure about only six of his men. That left five—including Spud—who he had not known much about before hiring.

"But Trevor knew 'em," Flood added, "at least, three of 'em."

"So he was confident about them?"

"Well, not really," Flood said. "He knew 'em, knew they'd worked other drives, but he hadn't worked with them himself."

"How did he get along with the three men?"

"Trevor didn't socialize with the men," Flood said. "I don't either. They worked for us, so we weren't lookin' to become friends."

"I understand," Clint said, "but that means we can't exclude those three men as suspects."

"I guess not."

Flood took Clint's empty plate and handed it to Spud, so the cook could finish cleaning up.

"Hang on to that coffee cup," he told Clint. "It's yours."

"Right."

They got up and walked to their horses.

"Hank, those three men have to be our top suspects," Clint said.

"That may be," Flood said, "but right now I just need them to be cowboys."

"If one of them killed Trevor, he may not be done," Clint said. "If his goal is to derail this trail drive, you could be next."

"Maybe his goal was simply to kill Jack," Flood said. "Maybe it has nothin' to do with the drive."

"That could be," Clint said, "but if you don't mind, I'm going to be cautious."

"If you're gonna watch those men, you'll have to watch all of them."

"I planned on doing that, anyway," Clint said. "I always watch the men around me. They may not all be happy that I'm here."

"I don't think any of these men are lookin' for a rep for killin' you, Clint."

"You never know, Hank," Clint said. "I've been shot at before by men who previously had no thought of a reputation."

"Okay," Flood said. "You watch the men, but make sure you watch my beeves, too."

"Don't worry, Hank," Clint said. "I intend to do my job."

Clint and Flood mounted their horses, followed by the rest of the men. Spud got his chuckwagon ready to travel while they all rode out to the herd. The biggest drive Clint ever went on was years ago, three thousand head. By comparison this thousand was a small herd, he knew that number could swell during the trip with the addition of strays.

He watched as the men circled the herd and started them moving. The first order of business was to ford the Red River. In the past many men and cattle had been lost to drowning in this river, probably the most treacherous of all the rivers they'd have to cross on this drive. They were either good enough or lucky enough not to lose any this time.

It must have been luck, because at that time nobody's talents stood out. The men all looked equally adept at what they were doing, but that could change on the trail. It didn't take much just to get a herd moving. In fact, sometimes it took more talent to get them to stop.

As Clint and Flood watched the men get the herd moving, they didn't know they weren't the only ones who were watching.

"Who's the new guy?" Larry Morgan asked.

"Clint Adams," Santiago Jones answered.

Morgan looked at Jones. The half-breed was a big man with a deep chest and broad shoulders. His black hair was cut very short, but he still wore a headband. Morgan knew that Jones had killed men in every way possible, including with his hands.

"The Gunsmith?"

"That's right."

"He's replacing Jack Trevor?"

"Yes."

"That's not good."

Jones shrugged.

"It won't be a problem."

"What about Trevor?"

"What about him?"

"Do we know who killed him?"

"I know."

"Who was it?"

Jones looked at Morgan. The man's stare made him feel cold.

"I know," he said, again.

"All right," Morgan said. "You and the others follow them. Do what you can to make sure they don't get where they're going.

# TWENTY-THREE

Crossing the Red River put them in Indian territory. In the old days an attack by Indians was always a possibility. It was much less so now, but there was always a chance of a small raiding party, so they had to keep alert.

Part of Spud's job as cook was to ride ahead of the herd, pick out a place for a campsite, and have a meal ready for the cowboys as they came in. After three days, about thirty miles, and three campsites Flood was satisfied that Spud knew his job.

After the same three days, Clint thought all the men seemed to know what they were doing. A few rode out in front of the herd, while the others either rode "flank" or "drag." One of them drove the "hoodlum" wagon, the one that carried all of the men's bedrolls. When driving a herd, men had to be able to maneuver quickly with their horses, which meant no extra weight on the animals, not even a bedroll.

Daltry, one of the men Clint had helped with the buckboard, was in charge of the remuda. He had to care for the extra horses and make sure they were always ready when a cowboy had to switch from a tired mount to a fresh one.

At night the job of watching over the herd was shared by everyone.

On the fourth night Clint and Flood sat off to one side, sharing their meal. They always ate away from the main body of men.

"Whataya think?" Flood asked.

"I've been watching all the men," Clint said. "Seems to me they all know their jobs."

"What if we mixed up their jobs?"

"What do you mean?"

"I mean a good drover, and professional waddie, can do any job on a drive. So we take the men riding flank and make them switch with the men who are riding drag. We make somebody else handle the remuda, and the hoodlum wagon.

"You want to switch somebody with Spud?" Clint asked.

"Hell, no," Flood said. "The man's a magician with the chuckwagon, and he picks out good campsites. I don't want to play around with him."

"That's fine," Clint said. "I'll start switching things up. If anybody doesn't belong he'll soon start to stand out."

"Good."

"Now what about the fact that we're being followed?" Clint asked.

"What?" Flood asked. "By who?"

"I don't know," Clint said. "I thought you'd be able to tell me who."

Flood stopped chewing and stared at Clint.

"Whataya mean by that?"

"I mean I think there's something you're not telling me, Hank," Clint said.

"Like what?"

"Like there's more to this last drive than meets the eye," Clint said. "Like maybe if you thought I knew I wouldn't have come along. Well, it's too late now, isn't it? I'm here."

Flood chewed and swallowed, washing it down with a swig of coffee.

"It's not too late," he said. "You could always leave."

"It's one of my faults, Hank," Clint said. "I always finish what I start."

"Okay," Flood said. "Okay." He put his plate down and stood up. "Let's go for a walk."

"Why?"

"Because I don't want to talk here," Flood said.

Clint frowned. If he didn't know Flood, and trust him, he wouldn't have agreed.

"Okay, Hank," Clint said. "Let's go for a walk."

"You ever heard of a man named Larry Morgan?" Flood asked, when they were between the campsite and the herd.

"That sounds like a pretty common name," Clint said, "but no, I haven't."

"He used to be a trail boss, like me," Flood said, "but lately, the last few years, he's gone rogue."

"Rogue?" Clint asked. "How does a trail boss go rogue?"

"Instead of headin' up a trail drive and a gang of drovers, he heads up a gang of killers."

"A private army?" Clint asked. "Mercenaries?"

"Not quite," Flood said. "They ain't that disciplined. They're just a bunch of killers. His segundo is a half-breed named Santiago Jones."

"Jones? That his real name?"

"Who knows?" Flood asked. "But the man is a killer, pure and simple. Worst of the bunch."

"And what does this all have to do with your last trail drive?"

"Morgan heard about it," Flood said. "He's determined to see that I don't get this herd to the end of the line."

"So he killed Trevor?"

Flood shrugged. "I don't know," he said. "Maybe. But he knows me well enough to know that wouldn't slow me down."

"So it still could have been something personal that got Trevor killed."

"Yup."

They stopped when they got to the point where they could see and hear the herd. There were several riders on watch, and Flood was thinking of increasing that number now that Clint told him they were being followed.

"We bein' followed, or watched?" he asked Clint.

"That's a good question," Clint said. "I haven't seen anybody, but it's not hard to follow a herd of a thousand steers. But it could be that we're being watched."

"Might not be Morgan," Flood said. "Might be rustlers."

"The last rustlers trying to steal steers from the last trail drive?" Clint asked.

"As if my life could get any more confused," Flood said. "I'm a man who doesn't like change, Clint, and there's lots of change comin'."

"I know how you feel," Clint said. The time was coming—and fast—when he and some of his friends, like Bat Masterson and Wyatt Earp, were going to be out of date. He wasn't looking forward to that, either.

# TWENTY-FOUR

Santiago Jones pushed himself back from the crest of the rise, so he could stand without being seen from below. The other two men with him watched and waited, but when nothing was forthcoming and the man continued to stand like a statue, one of them spoke up.

"Hey, Jones?" Bill Lacey said. "What's goin' on down there?"

"Nothing," Jones said. "They are camped for the night."

"The herd bein' watched?" Steve Peters asked.

Jones looked at him with cold eyes. "Of course, it's being watched."

"Why don't we just stampede it?" Lacey asked. "I mean, that would pretty much put an end to this drive. Ain't that what the boss wants?"

Jones looked at Lacey, who got the chills.

"I will decide what gets done, and when," he said. "Understood?"

"Yeah, sure," Lacey said, and Peters nodded. "You're callin' the shots, Jones."

"Yes," Jones said, "I am."

He walked down the hill. The other two men looked at each other, shrugged, and followed.

                              *   *   *

Clint decided to take a turn watching the herd before he
turned in. He wanted the men to see that he would be doing
the work as well as supervising them.

The sky was cloudless, the moon almost full. It was still
spring, although late. Most trail drives would have started
before now, but most trail drives were gone.

He sat high in his saddle, watching the surroundings rather
than the herd. Although there was bright moonlight, he still
couldn't see anything on the surrounding hilltops. He was
going to have to tell Spud to pick campsites on flatter ground.
That would make it harder to watch them.

He heard a horse approaching and turned his attention to
it. It was Roland, one of the men he'd helped load the buckboard back in Doan's Crossing.

"Nice night," Roland said.

"Good night for a stampede," Clint said.

"What?"

"It's quiet," Clint said. "Wouldn't take much to spook
this herd."

Clint had the feeling that both Daltry and Roland were
kind of new to the job. They seemed to know what they were
doing, but they just didn't seem to have been doing it as
long as some of the others.

"W-what would cause that?" Roland asked, thereby ad-
mitting his lack of experience.

"Almost anything," Clint said. "Big cats, snakes, shots, it
all depends on how the cows in front act."

"In front?"

Clint nodded.

"The natural leaders usually gravitate to the front of the
herd, so the rest of the herd goes the way they go."

"Geez."

Roland had been riding flank the first two days.

"I'm going to move you to the point, Roland," Clint
said. "Give you a chance to see what I'm talking about."

"Uh, we already got men ridin' point, Boss."

"That's okay," Clint said. "I'm going to make some changes from time to time. Give everybody a chance to move around."

"Uh-huh." Roland didn't look too happy with the news.

"Don't worry," Clint said. "By the time this drive is through, you'll know every job inside and out."

"Um, okay."

"And I'll know every man on this drive," Clint added, "inside and out."

# TWENTY-FIVE

The next morning Clint made wholesale changes. He left the drivers where they were. They usually worked in pairs on either side of the herd, kept the steers from spreading out too wide. But he moved flankers to ride drag, drag riders to the point, and pointers back to drag just to see how they'd perform. He left the remuda and the hoodlum wagon alone for the moment.

Flood and Clint roamed the herd, watching the steers and the men at the same time. They also watched their back trail and hillside they passed along the way.

At one point Clint came up alongside Flood and asked, "Who do you trust the most?"

"You."

"Besides me," Clint said, and then added quickly, "and besides yourself."

Flood thought for a moment.

"Bud Coleman," he said. "He's ridden with me before."

"Coleman," Clint said. "I know who he is. Tall man, in his forties?"

"Sits his horse kinda crooked, after all these years," Flood said. "He's pretty much in pain all the time."

"What from?"

"Bad hip," Flood said. "Got thrown a few years back, landed on it."

"You know, I noticed we had somebody who was struggling to keep up. Why don't we let him drive a wagon?" Clint asked.

"Because he's a trail driver and that's what he wants to do," Flood said. "He don't care how much it hurts."

"Well, maybe I can give him something to do that won't require so much cutting and turning."

"Like what?"

"Like checking to see if we really are being watched," Clint said.

"I ain't sure about that," Flood said.

"About what?"

"I don't think he'd be up to that."

"What are you telling me, Hank?"

"We're carryin' Bud, Clint," Flood admitted. "I wanted him along on this drive, but he ain't really doin' us much good."

"Okay, then," Clint said, "who's the second man you trust the most?"

During the course of the day, Clint watched Bill Coleman and saw what Flood was talking about. The man was so intent on not falling off his horse that he barely did any work at all. He would have been so much better off driving one of the wagons, but his pride would probably have hurt more than his hip did.

Flood came up with another name, a man called Chip Ryan. He said he'd used Ryan on a couple of drives, but that the man had a lot of other talents.

"What kind of talents?"

"You'll have to ask him," Flood said. "I don't know which ones he'd want to admit to."

"Okay," Clint said. "I'll do it at chow tonight."

So as the camp filled with the wonderful smells of Spud's

supper, Clint approached Chip Ryan, who was sitting with some of the other hands. They all stopped talking as Clint approached.

"'Evenin', Boss," one of them said.

"Good evening," Clint said. "Which one of you is Ryan?"

"That's me." A red-haired man in his thirties stepped forward. "What can I do for you, Boss?"

"You can come and eat with me," Clint said. "I have something to talk to you about."

Ryan looked confused.

"Am I gettin' fired?" he asked.

"No, no, nothing like that," Clint said. "I just have somethin' I want you to do for me."

"Like what?"

"We'll talk about it over supper," Clint said. "Join me by the chuckwagon in ten minutes."

"Yessir."

Clint turned and left, heard the conversation erupt behind him.

"Wonder what he wants you to do?" somebody asked.

"And why he picked you?" another said.

Let them wonder, he thought.

He joined Flood by the fire.

"I've asked Ryan to come and eat with us."

"With you," Flood said. "I'll take my plate over there, let you talk to him alone."

"All right."

"I hope you'll be able to trust him, Clint," Flood said.

"Yes," Clint said. "So do I."

# TWENTY-SIX

Chip Ryan got his chow from Spud Johnson, then walked over to where Clint was sitting with his plate and coffee.

"Pull up a crate," Clint said.

Ryan sat down, his movements very tentative.

"Relax," Clint said. "I told you you're not getting fired. Eat your supper."

Spud had created a combination of bacon, beans, and potatoes that lived up to his name. There were also some fresh biscuits that just about melted in your mouth.

"Flood tells me you're trustworthy, Ryan," Clint said. "What do you say?"

"I do my job," Ryan said.

"He seems to think you have other talents, though," Clint said. "You don't spend all your time working cattle."

"I've done other things," Ryan admitted, still not comfortable with the situation.

"Like what?"

"A little bit of everything," Ryan said.

"Okay, let me get to the point, Chip," Clint said. "Can you handle a gun?"

"Well . . . yeah. I've worn a badge a time or two, was a bounty hunter for a year or two. I can hit what I shoot at."

"How good are you on a horse?"

"Real good."

"Can you ride somebody's back trail without them seeing you?"

"Well, sure, but—"

"I think we're being followed," Clint said, "or watched. I want somebody to lay back and find out for sure. Is that something you think you could do?"

"That's what this is about?" Ryan asked.

"That's it."

He stood up.

"I'm gonna get some more of this chow. I'll be right back."

Clint watched as Spud spooned more food into Ryan's plate, and then the man came back, sat down, and started eating with gusto.

"You just about ruined my supper, Mr. Adams," Ryan said. "I didn't know what you were gonna say to me. Now that I know, I can enjoy my food."

"Well, I wasn't looking to ruin your appetite, Chip," Clint said. "I told you your job was safe."

"Yeah, well . . ."

"Can we talk about it now?"

"Sure, Mr. Adams," Ryan said. "I ain't especially fond of herdin' cattle. I was just doin' this for the money, and because it'd gimme time to decide what I wanted to do after."

"Well, what I want you to do is simple," Clint said. "You have to do it without being seen. If you don't think you can—"

"If I don't wanna be seen," Ryan said, cutting him off, "I don't get seen."

"Okay," Clint said. "I suggest you circle around for miles, then come back. That way if there's somebody, there you'll come up behind them. Even if they do see you, they won't connect you with the herd if you're coming at them from behind."

"Sounds good," he said. "When do you want me to go?"

"Well, that's the other thing," Clint said to the younger man. "Can you ride at night without breaking your neck?"

Ryan smiled.

"No problem."

After Ryan went back to the other men—with instructions not to tell them what he was doing—Flood came back over to Clint.

"What's the story?"

"He'll go out tonight, circle around, and see if we're being watched."

"Then what?"

"Then he'll come back and tell us," Clint said. "Is there anything distinctive about this fellow Morgan? I mean, if Ryan comes back and describes him will you know him?"

"Morgan's normal-lookin'," Flood said, "but Jones, now there's another story.

"So if he comes back and describes Jones . . ."

"Oh yeah," Flood said, "I'll know him."

"Okay, then."

Clint sipped his coffee and stared out into the distance.

"What's on your mind?"

"If we are being followed, and it's Morgan's men, and the point is to see that you don't finish this drive, why not just stampede the herd?"

"I dunno," Flood said. "Maybe they're worried some of my men would get killed."

"You really think that's a worry for Morgan?" Clint asked.

"No," Flood said, after a moment "I don't think that, at all."

# TWENTY-SEVEN

After dark Clint walked with Chip Ryan to where the horses were picketed, watched while the man saddled his horse.

"You sure you want to do this, Ryan?" Clint asked.

"You ain't tryin' ta talk me out of it, are ya, Boss?" Ryan asked.

"No," Clint said. "I just want you to know what you're getting into."

"All I'm doin' is takin' a ride," Ryan said, "and a look see. What harm can come from that?"

"None at all," Clint said.

Ryan smiled and mounted up.

"Just don't step in any chuckholes while you're at it," Clint said.

"Ol' Stony here is as surefooted as they come," Ryan said. "You don't have to worry about him steppin' wrong."

"That's good," Clint said. "I hope to see you this time tomorrow, Ryan."

"Twenty-four hours oughtta be enough, Boss," Ryan said. "Just have some of Cookie's coffee ready for me."

The men had already taken to calling Spud Johnson "Cookie."

"It'll be ready," Clint said.

Ryan nodded and rode out into the dark.

When Clint returned to the fire, Spud Johnson handed him a cup of coffee.

"Thanks, Spud."

"Somethin' wrong, Boss?" Spud asked.

"What makes you ask that?"

Spud shrugged.

"I just got a feelin'."

"Well, there's nothing for you to worry about."

"That's good," Spud said. "I don't want nothin' to go wrong with this job."

"Just worry about keeping the men fed, Spud," Clint said.

"Yessir." He looked over Clint's shoulder. "Coffee, Boss?"

"Yeah, thanks, Spud," Flood said.

The cook poured a cup and handed it to Flood, who nodded his thanks, again.

"Ryan get off?" Flood asked.

"Yeah."

"What are you so sour about?"

Clint looked at Flood.

"I'm thinking this should have been something I did myself."

"I need you here."

"I know," Clint said, "but if something happens to Ryan . . ."

"You give him a choice, or an order?"

"I gave him a choice."

"Then he knows what he's doin'," Flood said. "I wouldn't worry about it."

They drank their coffee in silence for a while, and then Clint said, "There is something else I'm worried about, though."

"What's that?"

Clint looked at Flood.

"I'm worried that there's still something you're not telling me."

Flood stared back at Clint, then looked down at his coffee cup.

"Spud?" he yelled.

"Boss?"

"We need some more coffee."

"Comin' up."

"And bring out that jug I give ya."

"Comin', Boss."

Spud came over with a big cast-iron coffee pot, and a bottle of whiskey that was still three-quarters full.

"My private stock," Flood told Clint.

Spud poured the coffee, and then topped it off with a finger of whiskey each.

"Thanks, Spud," Flood said.

"Sure, Boss."

Spud walked off with the pot and the jug.

"Drink up," Flood said to Clint.

"You thinking if I'm drunk enough I won't be mad at you when you tell me?" Clint asked.

"Tell me what?"

"Whatever it is you're going to tell me that needed whiskey."

"Maybe I needed the whiskey."

"Whoever needed it," Clint said, "what's going on, Hank?"

# TWENTY-EIGHT

"What makes you think there's somethin' I ain't tellin' you?" Flood asked.

"Because no matter how I look at it, it'd still be easy for somebody to stampede this herd," Clint said. "Then they could pick off whatever men weren't trampled. So there's something else going on here, something other than keeping you from completing this drive."

Flood studied Clint for a moment, and then sipped his spiked coffee before speaking.

"No, it's still about makin' me fail," Flood said, "but it's got to look like I failed on my own. See, Morgan is lookin' not only to stop me, but to humiliate me, too."

"They could still cause a stampede," Clint said. "It's happened on a lot of drives."

"I know it," Flood said. "And they still might try, but maybe they got a few other tricks up their sleeves, first."

"Like killing Trevor."

"Yeah, like that."

Clint studied Flood, and then said, "Hank, I can't help feeling like I've been suckered."

"Maybe ya have, just a little, Clint," Flood said, "but damn it, I need you. Some of these men don't care what my reputation is, but they'll care about yours. They'll do their jobs and maybe they won't run off at the first sign of trouble for fear that you'll go after them."

"So I'm here just to scare them into working, huh?" Clint asked.

"Maybe it started out that way," Flood said, "but now I need you. With Trevor gone, I needed a man I could trust. I mean, really trust to get the job done. Even if . . ."

"Even if what?"

"Even if I don't make it," Flood said. "I don't care what happens, Clint, this herd has to make it to Fort Laramie. You gotta promise me that."

"All right, Hank," Clint said. "I promise."

Clint looked out into the darkness, again.

"Okay," he said, "we'll know more when Ryan gets back here tomorrow night. For now let's just double up on night duty and tell the men to keep alert."

"Keep alert for what?" Flood asked.

"They don't have to know that," Clint said. "We'll just tell 'em to do their jobs."

Two of the six men who were riding with Santiago Jones for his boss, Larry Morgan, sat by their fire drinking coffee and looking at Jones, who was sitting off by himself, as he usually did.

"So, what's his story?" Zeke Sterling asked.

"Whataya mean?" Chris Dawkins asked.

"Well, they say he's a half-breed."

"So?"

"So does that mean he's part white, part Indian?" Zeke asked. "Or part white part Mexican?"

Chris thought a moment, then said, "I dunno. Maybe he's part Indian and part Mex. What's the difference?"

"I don't like half-breeds," Zeke said. "Can't trust 'em to pick a side, ya know? Ya never know when they'll turn on ya."

"Well, why don't you go over there and ask 'im, then?" Chris asked. "Tell him you don't like half-breeds and see what he does."

"Are you crazy?" Zeke said. "I don't wanna get myself killed."

"Then keep yer trap shut," Chris said. "Drink your coffee."

Santiago Jones had allowed his men to build a fire each night for two reasons. One, the smell of their camp would be swallowed up by the smells coming from the trail drive's camp. Second, he didn't really care if Flood and his men realized that Jones and his men were there. It would give the old trail boss something to think about.

Morgan's orders were that Flood and his steers didn't make it to Fort Laramie. He didn't care where along the way Jones stopped them, as long as he stopped them. And Jones didn't care what Morgan's reasons were. He was getting paid for this job, and that was all he cared about.

He might have made a move against the herd earlier—perhaps stampeding them—had Henry Flood not replaced Jack Trevor with the Gunsmith, Clint Adams. The presence of Adams made this job much more interesting to Jones.

The time of the trail drives and big herds may have been passing, but even more important to Jones, the time of the legends was passing. And any man who put an end to a legend would be remembered as a legend, himself.

So while he was determined to do the job he was being paid to do, he was going to do it in a way—and at a time—that suited his own purposes, as well.

# TWENTY-NINE

Clint used the next day to see how his experiment with moving the men around was going. But it was Flood who noticed the difference much before Clint did.

"Did you put Daltry on point?" he asked, halfway through the day.

"Yes, I moved a few of the men around. I wanted to see how well rounded they were."

"Well, he ain't," Flood said. "The man is scared to death to be out in front of this herd. Put him back on the flank."

"You're the boss."

Flood nodded, and then peeled off to ride toward the back of the herd.

During the course of the day Flood returned to Clint to order more changes. Before the day was over, men had been put back where they had been before Clint moved them. Flood had undone everything Clint had done.

If this had been Clint's regular job he would have bitched at Flood that night. There was no way he would have been able to do this job if Flood was going to undo everything. But this was Flood's baby, and Clint was just along for the ride, so he didn't object to Flood exercising his authority.

As Flood had said, Daltry was scared stiff to be in front of the herd and was much more comfortable riding flank—as was his compadre, Roland.

As they got on toward late in the day, Clint had to admit that Flood had done the right thing. The herd was moving along much better and strays were kept to a minimum.

That night the men were in a good mood, laughing and arguing good-naturedly while they ate. Clint and Flood sat together, quietly eating Spud Johnson's latest concoction of potatoes, meat, onion rings, and apples, which he called Range Riders Stew.

"You thinkin' about Ryan?" Flood asked.

"Yes."

"Me, too," Flood said. "Supposed to be back in twenty-four hours."

"That still gives him three," Clint said.

"I know," Flood said, "but I was hopin' he'd be back before then."

"So was I." Clint put his empty plate down, picked up his coffee cup. "I knew I should have gone myself."

"Can't start blamin' yerself at this point," Flood said. "Besides, I needed you here."

"I couldn't have done much more harm, if I'd been gone today."

"Don't sulk," Flood said. "So I had to make a few changes. So what?"

"I'm not sulking," Clint said. "I'm just saying I probably would have done more good—"

"Forget it," Flood said, cutting him off. "What's done is done. Ryan'll be back later. I'm gonna get me some more of this stew." Flood stood up. "Best idea you ever had, hiring Spud—and the men agree."

Clint agreed, too. Every supper they'd eaten so far had been a hit with everyone. Spud Johnson sure belonged in a chuckwagon more than he did behind the bar in a saloon.

Clint decided to get some more stew for himself, too, before the rest of the men started crowding around for seconds.

"I wonder what was goin' on today?" Al Swisher said aloud.

"Whataya mean?" Daltry asked.

"I mean with Flood and Adams," Swisher said. "Adams makes some changes, and the boss changes 'em back."

"I think they was tryin' ta prove who the real boss was," Eddie Pratt said.

"Naw," Roland said. "Not Adams."

"Whataya mean?" Daltry asked, again.

"Adams don't care who's boss," Roland said. "He helped me and Daltry load the buckboard at Doan's store the mornin' we left."

"And he takes his turn every night," Swisher pointed out.

"I heard them talkin' one night," Roland said. "Adams is just along to help Flood out, because Trevor got hisself killed in Doan's Crossing."

"Yeah, what was that about?" Swisher asked.

"Nobody knows," Daltry said.

"Maybe Jack slept with the wrong girl," Swisher said.

"I don't know," Pratt said. "I think somethin's goin' on that we don't know about."

"I don't wanna know about it," Daltry said. "That's why there's bosses, so they can worry about stuff like that."

"Damn, this stew is good," Swisher said, changing the subject. "That new Cookie is great . . ."

Roy Sobel, Bud Coleman, and some of the others were out with the herd. They'd be in later for their supper, changing places with some of these men.

Sitting off by himself, Andy Dirker kept quiet the whole time.

# THIRTY

By morning Chip Ryan had not returned. Clint and Flood were not happy. They scowled at breakfast, didn't discuss the matter. They both knew the chances were good the man was dead. Larry Morgan's men must have caught him and killed him.

Finally, breakfast done and Spud starting to load the wagon, Flood looked at Clint.

"What do we wanna do?" he asked.

"Let's get the herd moving," Clint said. "Once we're under way I'm going to go looking for Ryan. I'll slip away, using the herd to hide my movements."

"You think that's wise?" Flood asked.

"I sent him out there, Hank," Clint said. "I'm going to go out and find out what happened to him. And while I'm, out there, I'll have a look around." He pointed at Flood. "And I can promise you I'll be back by morning."

"With you gone I'll be two men short," Flood said. "Ol' Bud Coleman is gonna have to pull his weight, today."

"Let him handle the remuda," Clint said.

"That's a good idea," Flood said. "Okay, go ahead. We'll manage."

"I'm not going to let you know when I'm going," Clint said.

"I think I'll be able to tell you're gone," Flood said, sourly.

"You got a better idea, Hank?" Clint asked.

"Ah," Flood said, "I ain't mad at you, Clint. It's that goddamn Morgan. He just couldn't let me have this, could he? He's gotta make it hard."

"Well," Clint said, "maybe before this is all over, we can make things hard for him."

"Now that is somethin' I'd like to see," Flood said.

They saddled their horses, and as they mounted up Flood said, "You watch yerself and get your ass back here tonight."

"That's a promise," Clint said.

Clint was still hoping that Ryan would show up on his own, but by noon he hadn't, and Clint decided to make his move.

It wasn't unusual, during the course of the day, for a cowboy to peel off and chase down some strays, bringing them back to the herd. Or spotting some wild strays and collecting them to add to the herd. So Clint simply drifted off to one side, into the brush, and then just kept going.

Once he put some distance between himself and the herd he turned to check his back trail. If they were being watched and someone had noticed his move, they might have sent someone after him.

Eventually, he decided no one was following him. He turned Eclipse and started riding back the way the herd had come. Luckily, ten or fifteen miles a day is as much as a herd can cover each day. Retracing that with Eclipse would not take very long. He was going to circle, though, so it would take him a little longer. He wanted to get back to where they had camped two nights ago, which would be where Ryan had left them. From there he'd try to retrace Ryan's steps and find out what happened to him. Meanwhile, he'd do what he'd sent Ryan out to do in the first place, and see if they were being followed.

Right around midday Santiago Jones noticed something different. He turned and walked down from the rise he'd been using to watch the herd. His men were huddled together, waiting.

"Sterling and Dawkins."

"Yeah, Boss?" Dawkins said.

"Adams is gone," Jones said.

"Whataya mean, gone?" Sterling asked.

"He is not with the herd," Jones said, slowly. "Gone. See?"

"We see, Santiago," Dawkins said. "Whataya want us to do?"

"Locate him."

"And do what?"

"Nothing," Jones said. "I just want to know where he is."

The two men stood up.

"Where do we look?" Sterling asked.

"One of you ride on ahead, see if he went that way for some reason," Jones said. "The other ride back the way we came."

"Why would he go that way?" Sterling asked.

"Maybe," Jones said, "he's looking for us."

# THIRTY-ONE

Clint picked up a trail near their two-day-old campsite. He wasn't sure it was Chip Ryan's trail, but it was the only trail he had. While following the trail, he started to think he'd made a mistake telling Flood he'd be back by morning. At this rate he was going to have to make up almost thirty miles, and he wasn't going to be able to do a lot of it after dark.

He stuck to the trail for about five miles and then came to Chip Ryan's horse. It was lying on its side with a bullet in its head. Clint could see that the right front leg had been snapped almost in two. Apparently, despite all warnings, Ryan's horse had somehow managed to break a leg. It looked bad enough to have been violent, meaning Ryan may have been thrown when it happened. If that was the case then he was probably injured—but not too injured to have done the right thing by the horse. Plus, the saddle was gone, which means Ryan at least tried to carry it. How far was anybody's guess.

It was late in the day when Clint found out he had guessed wrong. He found Ryan's saddle lying on the ground. The saddlebags and canteen were missing, so at least the man was still trying to carry those—for another mile. At this point he was carrying only the canteen, which was probably not far from being empty.

Clint figured at this point there was an easy thirty miles between him and the herd—most of that covered by him and Eclipse. When he found Ryan, they were going to have to ride double. The big Darley Arabian would be able to handle it, but it would cut down on the ground they'd be able to cover. It would be late the next day by the time they caught up to the herd, unless he could find an extra horse.

Of course, there was always the possibility that Ryan was dead.

It was two more miles before Clint found out for sure.

Dawkins and Sterling had drawn straws to see who would ride ahead and who would retrace their steps. Dawkins ended up going back.

He and Sterling were not very smart, but they were each good trackers, which is why they had been hired by Santiago Jones. Each of the men he had hired—with Larry Morgan's money—were good at one particular thing. It was the only way to run a gang—don't hire anybody smart enough to want to try to take over.

He picked up the trail soon after he left camp, tracked it until it started to get dark. He didn't know what to do, then. Jones had not given him specific instructions on what to do when it got dark—camp, or keep tracking. He decided to camp, and since he had no specific instructions on what kind of camp to make—cold or not—he decided to make some coffee.

When Clint found Chip Ryan he was lying facedown on the ground. An empty canteen and his rifle were next to him. A stick he had probably picked up to use as a crutch was also lying next to him. His gun was still in his holster.

Clint dismounted, went to Ryan, and turned him over. He was still alive. He got his own canteen from his saddle, poured some water into his hand, and then slapped Ryan's face until he woke up.

"Wha—where—hey—"

"Here, drink some of this." Clint tipped the canteen up so Ryan could have a few sips.

"That's enough," Clint said. "Which leg hurts?"

"It's—It's my right foot."

"Just relax."

Clint checked the foot, found it swollen in the boot.

"Sprained, maybe broken," Clint said.

"Should we take the boot off?" Ryan asked.

"No," Clint said, "not till we get you back to camp."

"How are we gonna do that?"

"You, me, and my horse," Clint said. "Come on. Let's get you mounted, and then you can tell me what happened."

Clint got Ryan to his feet and they limped together over to Eclipse. With Clint's aid, he managed to get up in the saddle.

"Clint, thanks for comin' lookin' for me," Ryan said.

"How else was I going to yell at you?" Clint asked.

"Yell at me? For what?"

"I told you not to let your horse break his leg, didn't I?"

# THIRTY-TWO

Clint mounted up behind Ryan and then they started back. Ryan told Clint what had happened.

"I spotted our tail," he said. "Seven men, one of them was just watchin' the herd."

"Did you know him?"

"No."

"What did he look like?"

"Big man with a head band. Might be a half-breed," Ryan said.

"What'd you do then?"

"Well, I watched them for a while, then decided to come back. I had to circle around again, though, so they wouldn't see me. That's when my horse took a bad step, and I heard his leg snap."

Clint closed his eyes. He'd heard that sound before. It wasn't pretty.

"He step in a chuckhole?"

"No," Ryan said. "He just took a bad step."

That was the trouble with horses. They weighed about twelve hundred pounds or more and they carried it around on spindly legs. The slightest wrong step could cause a leg to snap. Eclipse weighed even more, and as strong as his legs were, they were still spindly. And now he was carrying two of them.

They rode for a while in silence, and then Clint reined Eclipse in.

"What is it?" Ryan asked.

"Coffee."

"You want coffee now?"

"No," Clint said. "Sniff the air."

Ryan did and he smelled it.

"Ah, coffee," he said, nodding.

Clint dismounted, handed the reins to Ryan.

"Stay here. Don't come unless I call for you."

"What are you gonna do?"

"Find out who's camp it is."

"You gonna kill him? Without knowing if he's part of the gang?"

Clint looked at Ryan. "Maybe not even then. Remember, don't come unless I call. And don't get down. Eclipse might kick you to death."

"I already feel like I've been kicked to death," Ryan said.

"Well, you haven't," Cling said. "Not yet. And if he starts to move, don't try to stop him. He'll know what he's doing."

He melted into the darkness.

Dawkins drank his coffee and cursed his luck that he was riding around out here on his own. He didn't know why they couldn't just ride ahead to Ogallala and wait for the herd there. They had enough men to make sure the herd never made it past there. And while they were waiting he could help himself to the best whores Ogallala had to offer.

He was about to pour himself another cup of coffee when he heard something—a boot scraping across a rock. He put the coffeepot down carefully rather than drop it. As he started to draw his gun, a voice said, "I wouldn't. You're covered."

Dawkins froze.

"What's the story, friend?" he asked. "I'm just sittin' here drinkin' coffee."

"I can see that," Clint said. "Why go for your gun, then?"

"Well, ya never know who you'll run across these days, do ya?" he asked. "Figure that's probably why you had your gun out, huh?"

"Yes," Clint said. "I like being real careful. What are you doing out here alone?"

"I was just thinkin' about that myself," Dawkins said, "I'm headin' for Dodge."

"Nothing much happening in Dodge, these days," Clint said. "What takes you there?"

"A job," Dawkins said.

"Doing what?"

"This and that. Just a job, and a look around at what used to be a hot town. I ain't never been to Dodge City before."

"How much coffee you got there?" Clint asked.

"Maybe a whole pot," Dawkins said. "You're welcome to some."

"I got a friend along."

"Bring him in."

Clint whistled loud enough for Eclipse to hear. He knew the horse would come running—well, trotting—and he hoped Ryan would remember not to fight him.

Finally, horse and rider came into the camp and Eclipse stopped.

Dawkins looked up at the new arrival, didn't know him.

"Have you ever seen this fellow before, Ryan?" Clint asked.

"No," Ryan said. "I don't know him." But then he looked over to where the man had secured his horse. "But I seen that pinto before."

"Where?" Clint asked.

"He was with those other men I seen watchin' the herd."

"Well, well," Clint said to Dawkins, "you're ridin' with a man named Santiago Jones, riding for Larry Morgan."

"I'm—I'm what?" Dawkins asked, nervously. "Naw, naw, I don't know them fellas."

"I'm going to ask you to drop your gun to the ground, friend. Nice and easy. Don't get brave and don't get clumsy. Either one will get you killed."

"I don't know what this is abou—"

"Just do it!"

"Sure, sure, mister," Dawkins said. "I'm doin' it."

Dawkins took his gun from his holster, briefly thought about trying to use it, and then realized that this was probably the Gunsmith. He dropped his gun into the dirt.

"Good boy," Clint said. "Now, my friend has a bad leg, so you're going to go and help him off his horse, take him to your fire and pour him and me some coffee. You got that? I'm going to watch you real close."

"Okay, mister, okay," Dawkins said. "I'm doin' exactly what yer tellin' me ta do."

"Keep it that way," Clint said, "and we'll all see the sun come up.

# THIRTY-THREE

Clint and Ryan were sitting on one side of the fire, with Dawkins on the other. The man had volunteered his name, but nothing else. Clint and Ryan were drinking coffee, and eating some beef jerky they'd found in Dawkins's saddle-bags.

"How about some of that for me?" Dawkins asked.

"Sure," Clint said, "just answer some questions."

"I can't."

"Sure you can," Clint said. "Tell me you work for Santiago Jones."

"I don't—I don't even know anybody named Jones," Dawkins said.

"Now that was a bad lie," Clint said.

Dawkins looked taken aback.

"Why?"

"Because everybody knows somebody named Jones," Clint said. He looked at Ryan. "Don't you know somebody named Jones?"

"Sure do."

"I do, too," Clint said. He looked at Dawkins. "See what I mean?"

"Okay, well, I meant I don't know anybody named—whatsit? Saint Jones?"

"Forget it, Dawkins," Clint said. "Your horse already gave you away. We know you work for Jones. What I want to know is, where's Morgan?"

"Morgan?"

"Is he with Jones and the others?"

"I don't know no Morgan."

"You're making this harder on yourself than it has to be, Dawkins," Clint said. To make his point he bit off a piece of beef jerky and washed it down with a swallow of coffee. "You know, you don't make bad coffee."

Dawkins bit the knuckle of his thumb. Thinking wasn't his strong suit.

"Come on, man," Clint said. "Talk or I'll leave you out here on foot."

"You can't do that!" Dawkins said. "I'll die."

"Yeah, you will."

"You wouldn't do that."

"I would."

Dawkins took off his hat and put his head in his hands.

"Ask me somethin' I can answer," he said, mournfully.

"Fine. Tell me you work for Santiago Jones."

Dawkins took his face out of his hands and looked at Clint.

"If I do you'll kill me."

"Not for telling the truth, I won't."

"Then he'll kill me."

"Well, now we're getting somewhere," Clint said. "At least you admit to knowing him."

Dawkins looked like he'd been tricked.

"I didn't say—"

"I tell you what," Clint said. "Would he kill you for telling us something we already know?"

Dawkins frowned.

"I guess not."

"Good," Clint said. "We know that Larry Morgan hired Jones and the rest of you to make sure Henry Flood's herd never gets to Fort Laramie. How am I doing so far?"

"Um, okay," Dawkins said, "except that Morgan hired Jones, and Jones hired us."

"See?" Clint said. "Now we're really getting somewhere."

He poured out a cup of coffee and handed it and a piece of jerky to Dawkins, who took it slowly, as if he was waiting for Clint to pull it back.

"Now," Clint said, "next question."

# THIRTY-FOUR

They tied Dawkins up for the night, took turns on watch. Ryan was feeling a bit better with some food and water in him. Clint took the second watch so he could let Ryan sleep a little longer. By the time he was ready to wake him he had anther pot of coffee going.

"Drink it quick," he said. "We've got to get moving."

Clint walked over and prodded Dawkins awake. The man hadn't really told them much. They tried to find out why Joncs was waiting, why he didn't just attack now and stampede the herd, but Dawkins told him he honestly didn't know.

"To tell you the truth, Mr. Adams," Dawkins said, "we was all wonderin' the same thing."

Well, Clint got the answer to one question. If Jones was making all the decisions, it probably meant that Morgan wasn't with them. He had either stayed behind, or gone on ahead. If he was intent on making sure the herd never got to Fort Laramie he was either there, or waiting at Ogallala.

Dawkins watched as Clint and Ryan broke camp, his hands and feet still tied. Soon it looked as though they weren't going to untie him. When they saddled Dawkins' horse and Ryan mounted up, the man knew.

"Hey! Ya can't just leave me here tied up!" he shouted.

"We aren't going to leave you tied," Clint said. "But we are going to leave you. We've got no choice. We've got to catch up to the herd."

"I'll die out here."

"I'll leave you one canteen," Clint said. "There's a waterhole about two miles back. We filled up there yesterday."

"And after that?"

"After that it's anybody's guess," Clint said. "I guess it'll depend on how bad you want to live."

Clint knelt down, cut the ropes on Dawkins's wrists and ankles.

"Damn, I can't feel my legs," Dawkins complained.

"Rub them," Clint said, mounting up. "They'll be fine in a while."

"Come on, Adams," Dawkins cried out. "Ya can't leave me like this."

"If you make it, Dawkins," Clint said, "think twice before you hook up with somebody."

As Clint and Ryan rode away they could still hear Dawkins shouting at them and, eventually, cursing them out.

Clint knew if he pushed Eclipse he could catch up to the herd before dark. However, the horse Ryan was riding would never have been able to keep up with the Darley Arabian. They were going to have to ride at the slower horse's pace. That meant they probably wouldn't catch up to the herd until the next day. By that time Flood would assume they were both dead.

They still had not tried to remove Ryan's boot. Once they caught up to the others they'd have to cut it off. Clint was starting to think they should have taken Dawkins boots, because Ryan was going to need a pair, but that would certainly have sentenced the man to death.

Clint considered riding up behind Santiago Jones and his men to have a look, but if they were spotted and got into a gun battle he wasn't sure how much help Ryan would take, and he didn't like the idea of six-to-one odds. So he decided to stay clear of them and ride wide around the trail left by the herd.

As it started to get dark Clint reined in and looked around.

"We better camp."

"I can keep ridin'," Ryan insisted.

"Maybe you can, but your horse can't," Clint said. "I'm not looking to ride the animal into the ground."

Clint got Ryan off the horse and seated, then went about setting up camp. They had Dawkins' coffee and coffeepot and the last of the man's beef jerky.

"But we could've caught up to the herd tonight," Ryan argued.

"Tomorrow will be soon enough," Clint said. "In fact, we might be able to catch up to them right around Dodge City."

"Maybe we can go into Dodge," Ryan said, his eyes brightening.

"I know what you're thinking," Clint said, "whiskey or a woman, but I'm thinking a doctor and a new pair of boots."

"Whatever," Chip Ryan said. "I'm thinkin' a cold beer."

"To tell the truth," Clint said, "so am I."

# THIRTY-FIVE

When Sterling returned with news that there was no sign that Clint Adams had gone on ahead of the herd, Jones assumed that Dawkins had found Adams and paid the price.

"What about Dawkins?" Sterling asked.

"Not back," Jones said.

"I can go look for him."

"Forget it," Jones said. "He probably found Adams, braced him, and paid the price."

"Why would Adams be goin' back?" Sterling asked.

"Don't know," Jones said, "but he won't be gone long. He ain't about to leave this herd."

"Why not?"

"Because he's not the kind of man who starts something and doesn't finish it."

"How do you know that about him?"

Jones gave Sterling a cold stare that sent a chill down the man's back.

"Because that is how I am."

Flood accepted a plate of food from Spud and then sat down to eat it alone. He assumed that Chip Ryan was dead, but he couldn't assume that about Clint. Something else must have happened to keep Clint from returning.

Someone approached, and when Flood looked up he saw Bud Coleman, plate and cup in hand.

"Hey, Boss."

"Hey, Bud," Flood said. "Have a seat."

"Thanks."

Coleman sat down, set his cup on the ground and started eating from his plate. He held his fork with his thumb on top and shoveled the food in.

"Thinkin' about Adams?" Coleman asked.

"Yep."

"Think he's dead?"

"No, I don't."

"Why not?"

"Because he's the Gunsmith, Bud," Flood said. "He'll be back."

"Well," Coleman said, around a mouthful of food, "if he don't make it back, I just want ya to know I'm ready."

"Ready?"

"To be segundo," Coleman said. "You're gonna need somebody to replace him, and the rest of these jaspers is either too young or too inexperienced."

"Well, you got a point there."

"I, uh, guess you noticed I ain't as good as I used ta be on a horse . . ."

"Really?" Flood asked. "No, I didn't notice."

"Well, it's true," Coleman said. "But I could sure do the job as segundo, Boss."

"Well," Flood said, "if Clint doesn't come back, I'll keep that in mind, Bud. Thanks."

"Sure, Boss," Coleman said.

He picked up his cup and went back to sit with the men and finish his meal.

"More coffee, Boss?" Spud asked, wielding the huge black coffee pot in both hands.

"Yeah, Spud, thanks," Flood said, holding out his cup.

"How about seconds on the stew?"

"Yeah, why not?"

He gave Spud his plate, and the cook returned with it filled.

"You really think Clint's not dead, Boss?" he asked.

"That's what I think, Spud," Flood said. "He's hard to kill."

"So whataya think happened?"

"He probably ran into some trouble," Flood said, "got a little farther behind then he thought. It'll just take him a bit longer to get back, that's all."

"I hope you're right, Boss."

As Spud walked away, Flood said to himself, "So do I."

Once again Clint took the first watch, determined to let Ryan rest as much as possible. He'd decided to push tomorrow so that they'd reach the herd before sundown. He wanted both horse and rider to have as much time as possible to regain their strength.

He was sorry to have left Dawkins on foot, but the man was healthy and he had every chance of walking to safety, as long as he didn't panic.

He decided that the most likely scenario in the minds of both Santiago Jones and his boss, Larry Morgan, was to stop the herd before they got to Ogallala, in Nebraska. That gave him and Flood some time to discuss their options. He didn't know how good Flood's hands were with a gun, but they could always turn and face Jones and his men. They had them outnumbered, but Jones and his men were gunhands. Experience was more important than numbers, unless you were talking about a huge difference. In this case they'd have Jones and his men outnumbered by two to one, but that would not make up for the fact that they'd be drovers against gunhands.

Of course, whatever he decided, Flood would have to agree. It was, after all, the man's last trail drive.

# THIRTY-SIX

Clint and Ryan started out early that morning, with intentions of catching the herd by nightfall. However, halfway through the day the pinto took a stumbling step and Ryan reined him in.

"He's gettin' tired," he said.

"I can see that. How about you?"

"Well . . . yeah, I'm gettin' tired, too. Maybe you should go on ahead."

"Chip, if I come back without you, then I might as well have not come at all."

"I guess."

"We'll slow down," Clint said, "and go back to the original plan."

They had discussed so many plans that Ryan was confused.

"Which plan was that?"

"We'll catch up to them tomorrow."

They continued on at a more sensible pace. Clint could feel the power of the Darley Arabian between his legs. The animal wanted to go!

"Maybe," Ryan said, "if we went in a straighter line we'd catch them faster."

"If we go in a straight line we'll run right into Jones and his gang."

"Who is this fella Jones?"

"Santiago Jones is a gunman, and the men with him are gunmen. That's why we don't want to run into them."

"I can handle a gun, Clint," Ryan said.

"I don't know that, Chip," Clint said, "and I'm not going against six experienced guns if I don't know that I can count on the man with me."

"I get it," Ryan said. "I understand. It'd probably be better if I could stand, right."

"I don't care if you can stand," Clint said. "I just have to be sure you can shoot."

"I can shoot better than any of the other guys—except maybe the old man."

"Flood?"

"No, not Flood," Ryan said. "Coleman."

"Bud Coleman?"

Ryan nodded.

"The man can shoot."

"How well?"

"He can hit anything he shoots at," Ryan said, no matter what size. A bottle, or a two-bit piece."

"Is that right?"

"Yeah."

"I didn't know that." Clint decided he better have a talk with Flood, and with Coleman, when they got back.

"What do you figure's goin' on?" Ryan asked.

"You don't know?"

"I figure Flood knows, and you know," Ryan said. "He don't confide in a bunch of drovers."

"Somebody's trying to keep him from finishing this drive."

"Why?"

Clint shrugged.

"Apparently somebody's jealous," Clint said. "Somebody else wants to have the last drive."

"This Jones?"

"The man he works for."

"Morgan?"

"Larry Morgan," Clint said. "Looks like he and Flood aren't exactly friends."

"I think Flood shoulda let on if there was gonna be trouble."

"You're probably right about that," Clint said, "but I think if he knew he would have hired some guns."

"He hired you."

"I'm not hired help, I'm doing this to help him out," Clint said. "And I'm not a hired gun."

"So you actually are working as his segundo?"

"That's right."

"But you'll use your gun if you have to, right?" Ryan asked.

"That's right."

"Then why don't you take out this Jones fella?" Ryan asked.

"He's got five other guns backing him."

"Use Coleman to back you."

"That's something I'm going to talk to Flood and Coleman about when we get back."

"Well," Ryan said, "if I can walk, I'll back your play."

"I appreciate it, Chip," Clint said. "I'll keep it in mind."

"Let's pick up the pace a bit," Ryan said. "He feels good underneath me, again."

"You sure?"

"Sure," Ryan said. "I know horses."

"Okay," Clint said. "Let's pick it up."

# THIRTY-SEVEN

Flood stared at the barbed wire that was, in effect, keeping him, his men, and his herd away from Dodge City.

"Boss?"

Flood turned and looked at Bud Coleman, who was sitting beside him on his horse.

"Why don't we just cut it down?"

"Because it's against the law, Bud," Flood said.

"But it's keepin' us from Dodge City."

"We're not goin' to Dodge City," Flood said, "but it is keepin' us from passin' near Dodge City."

"And it's keepin' us from goin' in a straight line," Daltry said. "What do we do?"

"The rest of you stay here," Flood said. "I'll try to reason with whoever put this wire up and see if they'll let us pass."

"This all used to be free range," Coleman said, shaking his head. "Now it's wired off. It ain't right."

"It may not be right," Flood said, "but it's progress."

Flood followed the barbed wire until he came to a gate. He was able to open it and close it without dismounting. He found himself on a road and followed it to a ranch house. It wasn't very large, but impressive enough. Built from local timber, two stories high, smoke coming from a stone chimney, and men with guns standing in front of it.

It was the men with guns that held Flood's attention.

He rode up to them, momentarily satisfied to see that no one had drawn their weapons.

"Who's in charge here?" he asked.

"That'd be me," an older, portly man said. He was holding a shotgun, with the barrels pointed down. "My name is Horace Bellows. I own this ranch."

"My name is Henry Flood."

"Flood," Bellows repeated.

"You've heard of me?"

"Not for several years," Bellows said. "Is that your herd adjacent to my land?"

"It is," Flood said. "We left Doan's Crossing with a thousand head. Must be about twelve hundred by now, with the strays we've been pickin' up."

"Too many," Bellows said.

"For what?" Flood asked.

"You're gonna ask me to let you drive your herd through my land."

"You're right," Flood said. "And what're you gonna say?"

"I already said it," Bellows replied. "There are too many."

"I won't let them graze," Flood said. "I just wanna drive them through. If I have to go around it'll cost me a day."

"That's why cattle are moved by rail these days, Flood. You're an anachronism, my friend."

"A what?"

"You're old-fashioned," Bellows said.

"Look," Flood said, "I'm just tryin' to make one last cattle drive. I'll pay you to let me drive them through."

"No deal," Bellows said. "They'll chew up my land with their hooves, and there's no way you can stop twelve hundred head from feeding if they want to. Go around, Mr.

Flood. In the big picture another day is not going to hurt you."

"Look, Bellows—"

The man raised his shotgun, and his ranch hands— twelve of them—drew their guns and raised their rifles.

"If you're looking for a fight you'll find one," Bellows said.

"I'm not lookin' for a fight," Flood said, wearily. He already had one brewing.

"Then go around, Mr. Flood," Bellows said.

Flood shrugged. He had no choice. He turned his horse and headed back to the herd.

When he reached the herd, the cows were anxious to be on the move. They smelled the grass on the other side of the barbed wire. If they didn't get them moving they might breach the barbed wire in their blind hunger.

He rode up to where Bud Coleman and the other hands were waiting.

"What happened?" Bud asked.

"We have to go around."

"Boss," Coleman said, "if we just let the herd go they'll head for the grass—"

"No, Bud," Flood said. "That'll start a range war we can't finish." Flood stood in his stirrups and shouted to his men, "We're goin' around!"

# THIRTY-EIGHT

Clint reined in Eclipse in front of the barbed wire.

"What happened?" Ryan asked.

"They had to go around because of the wire," Clint said. "We're going to run into more of that as we go along."

"What about Jones and his men?"

"I think they're behind the herd," Clint said. "We'll have to follow and look for an opportunity to rejoin the herd."

"What if they spot us?"

"If that happens," Clint said, "you'll get to prove what you told me about your shooting."

Ryan did not look as if he was looking forward to that.

"Come on," Clint said.

As they rode along the wire Ryan asked, "Do you think Flood asked the rancher if they could pass?"

"I'm sure he did, and I'm just as sure he was turned down," Clint said.

"Why?"

"Because no rancher wants better than a thousand head driven across his land. There wouldn't be much left for their own cattle."

"But Mr. Flood wouldn't let them graze, would he?" Ryan asked.

"You ever try to keep a thousand hungry cattle from eating? Can't be done. How's your foot, anyway?"

"Hurts like hell," Ryan said. "I think I need a doctor."

"There's a doctor in Dodge City," Clint said, "but not much else."

"I thought Dodge City was a great place to be."

"It used to be a great place and a dangerous place," Clint said. "Now it's neither."

"Should we go there for a doctor?"

"Let's catch up to the herd, first," Clint said. "Might be somebody there knows what he's doing. If not, then we'll go to Dodge if you still think you need it."

"What if my ankle's broke?"

"Not much a doctor can do but immobilize it and tell you to stay off it. Lots of people could do that."

"Like who?"

"There's usually somebody on a trail drive who can set bones, remove bullets, that sort of thing. Bud Coleman can probably do it, or Flood himself."

"Or you?"

"Or me."

Zeke Sterling was still upset that Chris Dawkins hadn't returned.

"He don't seem to care," he said, jerking his chin toward Santiago Jones.

"Why should he?" Frank Hughes asked. "We're just hired help to him."

"What about you?" Sterling asked. "Don't you care?"

Hughes shrugged and said, "Naw. I'm gettin' paid whether Dawkins comes back or not."

"You got any friends?" Sterling asked.

"No," Hughes said. "And I don't want any."

"Why not?"

"You can never tell when you might have ta kill a man," Hughes said, "even if he's yer friend."

He gigged his horse and rode away from Sterling, so the man couldn't talk to him anymore.

He looked around and saw Dale Bogard riding behind him.

"Hey, Dale," he said, dropping back, "don't you wanna go lookin' for Dawkins?"

"Hell, no," Bogard said. "Why would I?"

"Because he's one of us."

"Whataya mean, *us*?" Bogard asked. "I ain't no us, I'm, just me. If you got a complaint, take it up with Jones."

Like Hughes, Bogard rode away from Sterling, who wasn't getting any help from anyone.

Sterling thought about riding ahead, where Santiago Jones always rode alone, and complaining but he wouldn't have put it past the big man to kill him on the spot.

Sterling wanted this job to be over, wanted to get paid, and wanted to get away from Santiago Jones.

"What's wrong?" Ryan asked.

Clint didn't answer. He stood in his stirrups and looked around, then sat back down and looked down at the ground.

"We're right behind the herd," he said.

"So?"

"So nobody else is," Clint said. "I don't see any sign of Jones and his men."

"And that's a problem?" Ryan asked.

"They're not following," Clint said, frowning, "and from what I can see, they're not watching."

"Sounds like good news to me," Ryan said.

Clint was still looking at the floor, then turned his head and looked at Ryan.

"I can see where you might think that," Clint said.

"And?"

"Let's move."

Because Flood had to change direction with the herd, Clint and Ryan were finally able to catch up by nightfall. As they rode into camp the other hands went to greet them, shaking Clint's hand and slapping Ryan on the back.

"We thought you were a goner for sure," Ray Sobel said.

"He still might be," Clint said. "Help him off his horse and be careful with him. He might have a broken foot."

"How'd that happen?" Flood asked.

"I'll tell you all about it, but do you have somebody who can look at it?" Clint asked. "I don't want to have to go to Dodge City for a doc unless we have to."

"I'll have Bud look him over," Flood said. "Go get some coffee. I wanna hear all about it."

# THIRTY-NINE

Clint approached the chuckwagon and Spud Johnson stepped forward and held out a cup.

"Coffee?" Spud asked.

"And some food, if you've got some."

"Always."

Clint sat down and gratefully sipped the coffee. Spud brought over a plate laden with meat and vegetables.

"Couple of steer injured themselves and had to be put down," he said. "We had beef steak."

"Sounds good."

Clint was eating when Flood came walking over.

"Nice to see you back, Clint."

"You weren't worried about me, were you?" Clint asked.

"Naw, of course not," Flood said, accepting a cup of coffee from Spud. "You want to tell me what went wrong?"

Clint kept it concise, told Flood how Ryan had been injured.

"If you hadn't had to change course around the wire we'd probably still be trying to catch up."

"Yeah, that," Flood said. "You know, in the old days I woulda drove the herd right through that wire."

"I'm glad you didn't."

"I talked to the owner of the ranch. He and his men stood me off with guns."

"You were alone?"

"I wasn't lookin' for a fight."

"Still," Clint said, "it was my job to be with you."

"Maybe it was better that you weren't," Flood said. "It might have pushed those boys into using those guns. They were good men, backin' their boss. I wouldn't have wanted any of them to get hurt."

"You're probably right."

"What about our tail?" Flood asked. "I mean, if we even had one."

"Oh, you had one," Clint said. "According to Ryan's description Santiago Jones and six men have been trailing us. Then Ryan and I caught one of Jones's men and confirmed it."

"What happened to the man?"

"We needed his horse to get Ryan back here," Clint said. "We left him on foot with a canteen."

"Sounds good. Wait, you said we had a tail?" Flood asked.

"That's right," Clint said. "While we were riding back, trying to catching up, I noticed they were gone—no tracks, and so sign of them watching."

"So they're gone?" Flood asked. "They gave up?"

"Is Morgan the type to give up?"

"No."

"And I don't think Santiago Jones is, either," Clint said.

"Probably not," Flood agreed. "So what do you think happened?"

Clint chewed his food and washed it down with a swallow of coffee before answering.

"I think they've gone on ahead," he said. "Instead of following, they've decided to wait for us."

"Wait? Where?"

"My guess would be somewhere between here and Ogallala."

"Ogallala," Flood said. "Now there's someplace I haven't been in a while. I supposed it's changed as much as Doan's Crossing, Dodge City, Ellsworth, places like that."

"I suppose it has," Clint said. "But it's still the point where you steer the herd northwest to head for Fort Laramie. I think they're going to want to take their shot before that."

"Well," Flood said, "the good news is, we can stop watching our back trail."

"Yeah," Clint said, "but I think that's outweighed by the bad news."

# FORTY

Bud Coleman worked on Chip Ryan's foot, wrapped it, told him he couldn't walk on it, but he could ride. Flood found a pair of boots in the hoodlum wagon that were a couple of sizes too big, so he was able to get it on over the wrapping. Ryan needed only one boot—the right. After that he was able to work, but not walk.

They successfully worked their way around the barbed wire encircling the Bellows ranch, and got back on track. They had bypassed Dodge City, so they had no problems with hands wanting to go into town to get drunk.

They had a good month—give or take—before they would reach Ogallala. They didn't need the added annoyance of watching their back trail. They had trouble enough losing cattle to accidents and illness, losing a hand to an accident that never should have happened, and having to go around barbed wire several more times—one of which almost did escalate into a war. It was only the presence of Clint—introduced by Flood as "the Gunsmith"—that averted it.

To Flood's credit he never tried to push around the weight of his herd, or the weight of Clint's name. Each time they had to circle around land that was fenced in by barbed wire it cost them another day, but Flood did it. He didn't want it known that he shot his way through his last drive.

Ryan worked pretty well despite the injured foot, the other hands pulled their weight, but there was one man in particular who caught Clint's eye. He struggled to hold his own with the herd, and then in the evenings he sat off to himself while he ate. If he associated with anyone it was with Roy Sobel. Clint remembered that Sobel was the man Debra had told him about: aggressive, even violent, with women, and easily led by men.

The other man was Andy Dirker. If Sobel was being led then, it was by Dirker.

He started watching Dirker when one of the men's saddle slipped, causing him to fall under the herd and be trampled to death. Bud Coleman swore that the man's saddle had been tampered with.

Then, when the team pulling the hoodlum wagon got free, Coleman again said they'd been tampered with. Somebody was sabotaging the drive in small ways—except that the murder of Jack Trevor was no small thing. And he'd been stabbed. Clint noticed that, while he sat off by himself, Dirker had a habit of playing with his knife.

So unless Bud Coleman was the one committing sabotage, Clint's money was on Andy Dirker.

A week out of Ogallala, Clint brought the subject up to Flood as they ate.

"Dirker?"

"Did you know him before you hired him?"

"No," Flood said, "he's one of the men I hired toward the end, to fill out my crew."

"I'd like to find out some things about him," Clint said.

"Why don't you ask him?"

"I don't want him to know I suspect him."

"You got any idea who else you could ask?" Flood asked.

"I think I do."

"Who."

"Fella named Roy Sobel."

"Sobel," Flood said. "I've used him before."

"Somebody told me he was easily led."

Flood frowned, gave it some thought.

"I'd have to say that's true," he said, finally. "Seems to me whenever he gets in trouble it's because he was followin' somebody else. You think he's followin' Dirker? Helpin' him with the sabotage?"

"Maybe without knowing it," Clint said. "I guess I'll have to have a talk with him to find out."

"Let me know what happens," Flood said.

"I've got something else to talk to you about," Clint said.

"What's that?"

"Bud Coleman."

"You think Bud's involved?" Flood asked. "I don't believe that."

"No, I don't think he's involved, but somebody told me Bud can handle a gun."

"Was it me?"

"Somebody told me he can handle a gun real well."

Flood ducked his head, as if caught in a lie.

"Well, I didn't tell you that," he said, scratching his nose, "but it's true, Bud has a past he don't like to talk about."

"You think he'd back my play if I needed somebody?" Clint asked.

"Hell, I'll back your play," Flood said. "So will almost every man here."

"I need a man who can really use a gun," Clint said. "A man who's killed before. What about his past?"

"You'll have to ask him about it," Flood said. "It ain't for me to say."

"Okay," Clint said, "I can respect that. I'll talk to him about it."

"Good. I been thinkin' that even with the trouble we've had, this trip has been too good to be true."

"I think you're right, Hank," Clint said. "I think the worst trouble is still ahead of us, but let's see what we can do to head it off."

"I'm with you, Clint," Flood said. "Also, you've done a helluva job as my segundo. Just wanted you to know that."

"I appreciate it, Hank," Clint said. "I'm glad I could do a good job for you."

"Do you want to talk to Bud tonight?"

"I think I'd better," Clint said. "If Jones and his men don't try to spook the herd, it may come down to gunplay. I'll need to know who I can count on besides me and you."

"Okay," Flood said. "I'll send 'im over to talk to you."

"Thanks, Hank."

# FORTY-ONE

"Boss says you wanna see me?" Coleman asked.

"Have a seat, Bud," Clint said. He'd finished his meal and was drinking another cup of coffee. "Coffee?"

"Sure."

Spud came over and poured it for Coleman.

"We're heading for trouble, Bud, probably within the next week."

"I thought we were waitin' for trouble to come up behind us?"

"We were, for a long time," Clint said, "but now I'm thinking it's ahead of us."

"Whataya need me to do?" Coleman asked.

"I hear you're pretty good with a gun," Clint said.

Coleman frowned.

"Who told you that?"

"I just heard it."

Coleman shook his head.

"Somebody told you wrong."

"That so?"

"Yup."

"So you can't handle a gun?"

"As good as anybody here, I guess, 'cept you," Coleman said.

"That's too bad," Clint said, "because I think we're going to be going up against some shooters, and I'm going to need help."

Coleman didn't reply.

"Flood's going to be in trouble, too."

"Why's that?"

"He's going to stand with me," Clint said. "And if we have nobody else—"

"Stop."

Clint kept silent and watched the man. Coleman was working on something inside of him, trying to come to a decision.

"Okay," he said, finally.

"Okay, what?"

"Okay, I can shoot."

"When you say you can shoot . . ."

"I'm sayin'," Coleman replied, "that there was a time in my life when I was you, Clint Adams."

Clint was taken aback by that statement.

"What are you saying?"

"Oh, I don't mean I was anywhere near as famous as you," Coleman said, "but when I was in my late twenties I was feelin' my oats. I could outdraw any man alive—or so I thought. I could pretty much hit anythin' I shot at."

"So what happened?"

"I stopped," Coleman said. "I saw where I was headed, and I stopped. Started working cattle, kept my gun in the holster as much as I could."

Coleman had been looking into his coffee cup while he spoke. Now he looked up and locked eyes with Clint.

"I could have easily led the life you've led, although probably not as well," Coleman said. "I probably would've been dead by now—maybe even killed by you, at some point. Or, in any case, a better man."

"There's always a better man."

"You know that?"

"Of course I do," Clint said. "I hoping never to meet him, but I'm sure he's out there. . . somewhere."

The two men sat in silence for a few moments.

"So you've killed before, when you had to?"

"For a while I killed just because I could," he said, "but over the past twenty years or so—yeah, when I had to."

"So you can still use your gun?"

"That doesn't go away, Clint," Coleman said. "You know that."

Clint looked at Coleman's gun. He hadn't noticed before how well cared for it was. The man kept his weapon ready.

"Yeah, I know that."

"So what are we gonna do?"

"As we approach Ogallala I think you, me, and Flood should ride ahead."

"So you think they'll wait for us?" Coleman asked. "They won't circle back around us and stampede the herd?"

"They could have stampeded the herd at any time," Clint said. "I think Santiago Jones wants to face me, not trample me to death."

"I haven't heard of him before."

"Neither have I," Clint said. "Maybe he wants to change that."

"How many men has he got?"

"He had six, now he has five with him."

"So two-to-one odds," Coleman said. "I've seen worse."

"So have I."

"Maybe we can leave Flood behind," Coleman said. "Maybe you and me can handle it."

"You think so?"

"Yeah."

"You're not just trying to keep him safe?"

"Well . . . yeah."

"We probably should let Flood make that decision himself."

"Yeah, okay," Coleman said, standing up. "I'll keep working the herd until you need me. Unless there's somethin' else?"

"There is one thing."

"What's that?"

"How much do you know about Andy Dirker?"

"Not much, but I don't like 'im."

"Why not?"

"Keeps to himself," Coleman said. "Can't trust a man who does that."

"He's got no friends on the crew?"

"No," Coleman said. "The only one he talks to is Sobel, but they ain't friends."

"What about Sobel?"

"What about him? He ain't got a mind of his own, has to be told what to do."

"And has Dirker been doing the tellin'?"

"What are you gettin' at?"

"Back in Doan's Crossing Jack Trevor was killed with a knife. One like Andy Dirker's got."

"He's always playin' with that knife. You think that sonofabitch killed Jack?"

"Maybe. I want you to do something for me. Get a look at the bottom of his boots."

"What am I looking for?"

"A shape," Clint said, and explained what he had seen in a boot print in the livery where Trevor had been killed. "You see it, let me know."

"Okay," Coleman said. "I'll let you know."

Coleman walked away, his crooked gate betraying the problem with his bad hip.

# FORTY-TWO

Lawrence Morgan—who preferred to be called Larry by everyone, not just his friends—smoked a cigar while he watched the whore undress. He had chosen very carefully, sure to end up with the best-looking woman in the house. She was dark-haired, tall and slender, with very long legs and breasts like ripe peaches.

Morgan had been in Ogallala years ago when it was a town that lived off the cattle drives. Now—like Doan's Crossing, Dodge, and many others—it lived off crumbs.

That's what Henry Flood was trying to bring to Ogallala, the crumbs of his last cattle drive. Morgan hated Flood, always had. He'd spend his last dime if he had to, to make sure Henry Flood failed.

The whore dropped her see-through black-lace robe to the floor and stood before Morgan naked, still wearing her high heel shoes. Her skin was very pale, her nipples very dark brown, her breasts high and firm. He put his cigarette out and held his arms out to her. She came to him, crouched down in front of him, between his legs. He was naked, his erection standing out from an almost obscenely hairy crotch. None of the girls wanted to go with him because he was an ugly man—big, blocky, with abnormally large facial features.

This whore—Gloria—had gone with him because she was curious. His ears, nose, lips, and hands were so large she wondered what else he had that was large. Gloria loved a man with a large penis, and Larry Morgan's stood out like a miniature redwood.

"My God," she said, taking his huge cock in her hands.

"You like that, huh?" he asked.

Morgan knew he was an ugly man, but had been with his fair share of women and knew that what he had appealed to some. Some had been scared off by his features, and still others who had gotten as far as this—naked in a room with him—and then been frightened off.

But not this whore. Her eyes were shining as she stroked him, making him even larger.

"If we're not careful," she said, "you're gonna tear me up, leave me limping for days."

"Well, honey," he said, "we'll just have to be careful, won't we?"

Morgan didn't want to cause any trouble in town. He just wanted to be there when Santiago Jones came and told him that Henry Flood had failed. He was just killing time with this whore, so he was in no hurry. Let her spend as much time as she wanted ooh and ahhing over his cock.

"Well," she said, licking her lips, "let's see if I can get this monster into my mouth, and we'll just go from there."

"That's fine with me—" he said, but she cut him off by—amazingly—swooping in, opening her mouth, and taking him inside.

Santiago Jones liked this better.

Let Adams and Flood bring the herd to him. What was the point of stampeding the steers when they could keep them altogether and then take the herd for themselves after they killed Flood and Clint Adams?

The other men were milling about camp, looking for

some way to while away the time. None of them had the big half-breed's patience.

"Sterling," Jones called.

Finally, Sterling thought, Something to do.

"Yeah, Boss?"

"Ride back, see what you can see."

"Sure, Boss."

"If you spot them don't do a thing. Just come back and tell me. Understand?"

"Sure, Boss, I understand," Sterling said, "but once we spot them, what're we gonna do?"

"We'll ride out and give them a welcome," Jones said. "One they won't forget."

# FORTY-THREE

Days later Clint and Flood were riding together in advance of the herd.

"Well now," Flood said. "This looks familiar."

"It does?" Clint asked. "Can you tell how far out of Ogallala we are?"

"'Bout three days," Flood said.

They had been on the trail a little over two months. Once they reached Ogallala they'd still have about two weeks to go before they reached Fort Laramie.

"Might be time for us to ride up ahead," Clint said. "You, me, and Bud."

"Okay."

"But if we do that," Clint said, "who are we going to leave in charge of the herd?"

Flood frowned.

"Can't think of anybody I'd trust," he admitted.

"I can't either, Hank," Clint said. "Maybe you should stay, let me and Bud go ahead."

"And fight my fight?"

"I think the herd might be more important than your fight," Clint said. "Bud's going to back my play—"

"You never let anybody back you if you haven't seen

them in action before," Flood said. "I'm the only one that qualifies."

"That's true," Clint said, "but this is different. Somebody's got to stay with the herd, and the men, unless . . ."

"Unless what?"

"Unless we resolve the question of who in our camp is working for Morgan."

"You said you thought it was Dirker."

"I'm pretty sure, but I need one last piece of evidence."

"When will you get it?"

"Any time now, hopefully."

"Let's do this tonight, Clint," Flood said. "Let's brace him tonight and get it over with."

"Still doesn't answer our question of who we can leave in charge of the herd."

"Maybe we can answer all the questions tonight," Flood said.

"Except the last one," Clint said.

"That one," Flood said, "might get answered in Ogallala."

That night Clint and Flood decided not to do anything until after chow. They were eating when they heard the shots. The both jumped to their feet, plates and cups flying. They ran over to where the men were eating. The drovers were all on their feet, but Bud Coleman was the only one holding a gun.

"What the hell happened?" Flood demanded.

Clint saw one man lying on the ground. It was Andy Dirker. He was dying on his back, and Clint could see the bottoms of both boots. He walked over to check the body. Dirker was dead, two holes in his chest. Clint then checked the boots. There was no doubt Dirker's boots had left the marks on the floor of the livery where Jack Trevor had been stabbed to death.

"He did it," Coleman said. "He killed Jack. They all heard him say so."

Flood looked around.

"Is that true?" he asked the others.

"We heard Bud accuse him," Eddie Pratt said.

"Anybody hear Dirker admit it?" Flood asked.

"He's got the mark on his boot," Clint said.

"He went for his gun," Swisher said.

"What?" Clint asked.

"I didn't hear him admit to killing Jack, but when Bud braced him Dirker went for his gun. Bud outdrew him slicker'n snot."

Clint looked over at Roy Sobel.

"What about it, Roy?" he asked. "You know anything about what happened in Doan's Crossing?"

Sobel didn't answer.

"Come on, Roy," Bud Coleman said. He was still holding his gun.

"Okay, okay," Sobel said, "I knew somethin' was up in Doan's Crossing but I didn't know what. He went off by himself."

Flood looked at Clint.

"If he went for his gun when Bud braced him . . ."

"But we don't know if he was working for Morgan or not," Clint said, so the other men couldn't hear.

"I think Bud did the fight thing," Flood said.

"Okay," Clint said.

"Swisher, take some men and bury Dirker. Take whatever personal effects he has and put them in his saddlebags. We'll give it all to the law in Ogallala." He looked at Coleman. "Bud?"

Bud replaced the empty shells in his gun, holstered it, and followed Clint and Flood back to the chuckwagon.

"What happened?" Clint asked.

"I saw his boot, and like you said, there was that mark. I

got mad and accused him of killing Jack. The others didn't hear him, but he said, 'So what? What are you gonna do about it?' I said I wanted his gun and his knife. He underestimated me and went for his gun. That's it."

"What about Sobel?" Clint asked.

"He ain't involved at all," Coleman said. "I'm sure of it."

Clint looked at Flood.

"Hank, I guess you'll be staying with the herd tomorrow." He looked at Coleman. "I think Bud and I will be able to handle this tomorrow."

Flood looked at Coleman.

"I think that's best, Boss."

"Okay," Flood said, "somebody's gotta stay with the herd and I guess I'm the logical one."

"You and me, Bud," Clint said. "We'll leave at first light."

"I'll be ready," Coleman said.

# FORTY-FOUR

Santiago Jones was ready.

Sterling had returned the day before, saying that the herd was approaching, would probably arrive within a day. Jones didn't know what Flood and Clint Adams would decide to do. Whether they came ahead, or they came with the herd, they had to come through this pass, where Jones and his men were waiting. If they had they could stampede the herd once it was in the pass. If they did that, the drovers would have no chance to survive.

Under normal circumstances Jones wouldn't care how many men he killed, but this time he was only concerned about one—Clint Adams. As long as he killed him, and stopped the herd from reaching Ogallala, he didn't care if the other men survived or not.

Except for Flood. Probably the best way to stop the herd was to kill Flood.

He'd be the man who killed the Gunsmith, and the man who stopped Henry Flood's last trail drive.

Clint and Bud Coleman had coffee with Henry Flood, but no breakfast.

"I'd hate to get killed on a full stomach," Clint said.

Coleman didn't eat because it had been a long time since he did this sort of thing. Killing Dirker the night before had been instinctive—proving that he still had the reflexes to kill—but that didn't mean he had the stomach to kill.

Flood ate hungrily.

"If this is my last day on earth," he said, "I wanna have a full stomach."

Clint and Coleman saddled their horses and walked them over to the chuckwagon, where Flood was still eating.

"Just follow us in, Hank," Clint said. "We should have the way cleared for you."

"You sound sure of yourself."

"Well, whether we're dead or they're dead, they shouldn't be in any shape to stop you."

"Well, I hope it doesn't come to that," Flood said. "Good luck to you both."

"Thanks."

"Thanks, Boss," Coleman said.

Clint and Coleman rode out of camp.

"Think they're waitin' for us?" Coleman asked.

"I'm pretty sure they scouted us," Clint said. "They probably know we're coming."

"So how do we play it?"

"Head on," Clint said. "That's the way I usually play it."

"Maybe I should circle around—"

"That would take a while," Clint said. "I'm sure they're going to be waiting at Platte Pass. That's the best place to stampede a herd, if that's they're plan. But whether we showed up with the herd or without, we'd have to go through that pass to get to town. Besides, I'm pretty sure head on is the way Santiago Jones is going to want to play it."

"How can you be sure?"

"Once he heard I was along he started thinking like everybody else. Kill me for the reputation it would get him.

That's why he didn't stampede the herd before now. He wants to kill me himself."

"So you'll take him and I'll take the other five?" Coleman asked.

Clint laughed.

"No, Bud," he said, "I think we'll divvy it up a little more evenly than that."

"Want me to go have a look, Boss?" Sterling asked Santiago Jones.

"No," Jones said. "He's comin'."

"How can you be sure?"

"The herd's a day away," Jones said. "Adams won't wait. He'll come."

"How do we play it?" Sterling asked. "We can put a couple of men behind these rocks—"

Jones swung his massive left arm and knocked Sterling out of his saddle. The man hit the ground hard, rolled over and stared up at his boss.

"This is Clint Adams we're talkin' about," Jones said, looking down. The other men had noticed what happened and were listening and looking. "He deserves a better death than bein' ambushed. We face him head on, and you keep your eyes on me." He looked at the other men. "All of you. Do you hear?"

The other men nodded.

"You watch me for my move," Jones said. "I'll be first."

Frank Hughes came over and helped Sterling to his feet.

"What makes you think Adams is gonna give you the first move?" Hughes asked Jones.

"Because that's what he does," the half-breed said. "That's what he always does. He gives his opponent the first move— and that's gonna be his death, because when I have the first mover, I can't be beat."

None of the men knew this. They knew Santiago Jones

could kill most anybody with his bare hands, but they had never seen him use his gun.

"Okay," Hughes said, "I guess we have to take your word for that."

"Yeah," Jones said, "you will."

# FORTY-FIVE

Santiago Jones spotted them from well off.

"Two riders!" he called.

Behind him Frank Hughes sidled up next to Zeke Sterling.

"This whole thing don't make no sense," he said. "Why didn't we just stampede the damn herd when we had the chance—and we had a lot of chances!"

"Who know?" Sterling said. "Jones is the boss. You wanna tell him you don't agree?"

"No," Sterling said. "But that don't mean we gotta wait for him to draw. We can get the jump on Adams and whoever he's bringin' with him."

"There's six of us and two of them," Sterling said. "We should just play it the way Jones wants—otherwise you gotta deal with him after."

Hughes looked over at the other men.

"Or get one of them to go along with you."

Hughes made an annoyed sound and went to talk to the others.

"I see them," Clint said.

"I don't," Coleman said. "My eyes ain't what they used to be."

"Looks like six men, all on horseback."

"We gonna do this on horses?" Coleman asked.

"My guess would be we'll start on horseback," Clint said. "Once the shooting starts everybody's going to take off for cover."

"Hmm."

"What is it?"

Coleman looked at him.

"With my hip the way it is I ain't gonna be able to jump off this horse."

Clint thought a moment.

"I'm going to get off mine as fast as I can," he said, "and get him out of the line of fire. Is this a regular mount for you?"

"Naw, just a horse I took from the remuda."

"Good," Clint said. "When the shooting starts just turn the horse sideways and slide off behind it."

"I'll try," Coleman said.

"Just don't get dragged, Bud."

Coleman rolled his eyes.


"Okay, get up here," Jones called. "Fan out on either side of me."

The other men all mounted up and obeyed. Frank Hughes couldn't get any of the other men to go along with his plan, so he didn't know what he was going to do.

"Adams is mine," Jones said. "I don't know who the other man is, but he's yours."

"All of us?" Sterling said.

"Yeah."

"And after we kill him?" Hughes asked.

"Nobody shoots Adams," Jones said, "unless he kills me. Then he's all yours."


As Clint and Coleman approached the mouth of the pass the six men fanned out. Jones had two men on his right, three on his left. Clint wondered if it would have been a good idea to bring Chip Ryan along. The younger man might have been good enough with a gun. On the other hand he was still gimpy with a bad foot and, once they all got down off their horses, Ryan would have been at a disadvantage, like Coleman.

They stopped about twenty feet from the six men.

"Adams?" the big half-breed said.

"That's right," Clint said. "You must be Santiago Jones."

"That's me." Jones made a show of looking past Clint. "No herd?"

"It'll be along," Clint said. "I wanted to have time to move the bodies."

That made the other men stir. Clint knew he sounded confident, and that usually bothered people who had bigger numbers on their side.

"That's funny," Jones said, without a smile. "I've got an idea, Adams."

"What's that?"

"Why don't we step down from our horses and settle this between us."

"That sounds good to me."

"Your man will stay out of it?" Jones asked.

"He will. And yours?"

"They will, too."

"Okay, then," Clint said. "Step down."

"Is he serious?" Coleman asked.

"No," Clint said. "Watch the others. They'll draw, for sure."

"Can you take him?" Coleman asked, as Clint dismounted.

"I don't know," Clint said. "Remember, turn your horse and stay behind it."

"Okay."

Clint turned to Eclipse and slapped him on the rump. The horses scampered away, not too far, but out of the line of fire. When he turned Santiago Jones was standing on the ground with his legs spread.

Clint noticed something helpful. The five riders standing behind Santiago Jones were confused. They had obviously received one set of instructions, but now the big man had gone off on his own. They were looking at each other, wondering what to do.

He turned his attention to Jones.

"Where's your boss?" he asked.

"That doesn't matter," Jones said.

"Yeah, it does. I'm going to go and see him after I kill you."

"Ogallala," Jones said. "Give him my regards . . . if you get there."

The big man went for his gun, and Clint was surprised at how fast he was. In his experience, big men were not usually very fast. Against anyone else, Jones would have had a chance. He almost cleared leather when Clint shot him in the biggest target presented to him—the man's big chest.

Clint immediately turned to the five men on horseback. Coleman had already started shooting, and two men came out of their saddles as if they had been snatched from behind. He fired, taking another man from his saddle, and by the time the other two men realized what was happening, they were dead.

Clint quickly turned his attention to Coleman. As it turned out the older man had done most of his shooting while hanging over the side of his saddle. He was still on horseback.

Clint ejected the empty shells and replaced them as he walked to the bodies. He checked each one in turn, and they were all dead.

He turned and walled to Coleman, who was almost reloading.

"You hit?" he asked.

"No. You?"

"No."

"I was wrong," Coleman said.

"About what?"

"I once told you that years ago I was you," Coleman said. "I saw what you just did. Jones was fast, but I've never been and have never seen anything as fast as you."

Clint whistled and Eclipse came trotting over.

"We going to Ogallala to see Morgan?"

"No," Clint said. "I don't want to rob Henry Flood of that pleasure. We'll head back to the herd."

"Suits me," Coleman said. "Suits me just fine."

"Let's move these bodies," Clint said. "I don't want the herd to trample them."

"Should we take them all into town?"

"I think when we get here with the rest of the men we'll bury them," Clint said. "If the law in Ogallala doesn't like it, let him come out and dig them up."

"That suits me, too."

# FORTY-SIX

They forded the South Platte and then North Platte rivers the next day, then left the herd just west of town while Clint, Flood, Coleman, and Chip Ryan rode into town the following morning. Ryan was going to see the doctor while they were there.

Clint rode over to the doctor with him, while Flood and Coleman went to the saloon.

"I'm heading to the sheriff's office," Clint told Ryan as he dismounted. "See you there, or the saloon."

"Which saloon?"

"Probably only a couple left," Clint said. "The biggest one."

"Gotcha."

Ryan started for the doctor when Clint looked at the ground and saw the man's boot print. There was an odd design in the dirt.

"Ryan!"

"Yeah."

"That print," Clint said, pointing. "That the boot you got from the hoodlum wagon for your hurt foot?"

Ryan peered down at the ground, said, "Oh, yeah."

"What happened to the other one?"

"Dirker took it, said he needed a new boot."

"And how did those boots get into the wagon on the first place?"

Ryan shrugged and said, "Somebody said they were Flood's extra pair."

Clint nodded.

"Okay, go get your foot looked at."

Ryan headed for the doctor's office, while Clint went to the sheriff's office, shaking his head.

Clint and the sheriff found Flood and Coleman in the Driver's Saloon. Flood was bracing Larry Morgan. The two men were facing each other in front of the bar, both red-faced from shouting. It looked as if gunplay was inevitable, until Sheriff Rance Howard stepped in.

"I need you to come with me, Mr. Morgan," Sheriff Howard said.

"What for?"

"We need to talk about a man named Santiago Jones."

Morgan frowned.

"I don't know where—I mean, who that is—"

"We know where he is, sir," Howard said. "In the ground, along with the other men working for you. Now come along with me. I'll have that gun."

Morgan glared at Henry Flood while he handed over his gun.

"See you in Fort Laramie, Morgan," Flood said. "Oh, wait, you won't be there."

The sheriff marched Lawrence Morgan over to his office.

"Good thing you came in when you did, Clint," Flood said. "I woulda killed him."

"How, Hank?" Clint asked. "With a knife or a gun?"

Flood frowned.

"Whataya mean—"

"Your boots, Hank," Clint said. "You should have burned them, or buried them, not put them in the hoodlum tent."

"What's this about?" Coleman asked.

"The boot you saw Andy Dirker wearing was Flood's," Clint said. "Chip Ryan has the other one on his hurt foot. After Flood killed Jack Trevor he put those boots in the wagon and put on a second pair. When somebody grabbed one of them for Ryan, he couldn't object. And then Dirker grabbed the other one."

"So Dirker didn't kill Jack?" Coleman asked.

"No," Clint said. "He was probably following Hank and Jack around town, looking for a chance to do something that would sabotage the drive. But he didn't kill Trevor. Hank did. Dirker might even have seen him do it."

Coleman looked at Flood.

"That true, Boss?"

Flood shook his head, but he wasn't saying no.

"That Trevor, he wanted a bigger piece of the action. My last drive, and he wanted to horn in. I couldn't let him."

"I don't see why not, Hank," Clint said. "It sure would have been easier, don't you think?"

"How could you do that to Jack?" Coleman asked.

"Sorry, Bud." He looked at Clint. "The sheriff?"

"Oh, he'll be back. I asked him to give me time to talk to you."

"Clint—"

"What? Let you go? I can't do that."

"No," Flood said, "I wasn't gonna ask for that, but . . . could ya finish the drive? Take the herd to Fort Laramie? Pay the men off. Finish my last drive?"

"I can't do that either, Hank," Clint said. "It just wouldn't be right."

"No," Flood said. "No, I guess not."

At that moment the sheriff came walking back in.

"Is he ready?" he asked Clint.

"Those stupid symbols on the bottom of my boots," Flood said. "An old habit, just to identify my property. Learned it when I was a kid."

Clint plucked Flood's gun from his holster, tossed it to the lawman.

"He's ready."

As the sheriff led Flood out of the saloon, Bud Coleman said, "Jesus."

"Have a drink with me, Bud," Clint said.

Clint didn't drink whiskey often, but this seemed like on occasion to have a shot.

"What do we do now?" Coleman asked, when they each had a drink.

"Finish the drive."

"But you said—"

"I said I wouldn't finish the drive for Flood," Clint said. "But we can finish it, and instead of paying the men off you can all have an equal share."

"What about you?"

"I don't want any money," Clint said. "I'm going to chalk three months work up to experience. You and the men can split it."

Bud Coleman lifted his glass of whiskey and said, "That works for me."

Watch for

**THE HUNT FOR CLINT ADAMS**

343rd novel in the exciting GUNSMITH series
from Jove

*Coming in July!*

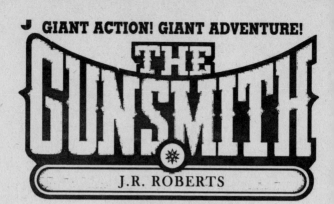

GIANT ACTION! GIANT ADVENTURE!

# THE GUNSMITH

## J.R. ROBERTS